It's late January and Loon Lake is hosting an International Ice Fishing Festival. Police Chief Lewellyn Ferris and her limited team are busy with the usual headaches and then some, and Doc Osborne is busy studying fly-casting videos in an effort to impress Lew come spring.

But a panicked call from Rob Beltner leads to a sad discovery: his wife, Kathy, is dead of a gunshot wound. Lew barely begins to investigate the shooting before she's sidetracked by the imposing figure of Patience Schumacher, president of Wheedon Techincal College. Patience is certain she's being stalked, and as Lew investigates, the uncanny coincidences accumulate like snow on the frozen, deadly surface of Loon Lake ...

Victoria Houston fishes and writes in northern Wisconsin. Along with her critically acclaimed Loon Lake mystery series, she has written several non-fiction titles. Visit www.victoriahouston.com for more information.

DEAD DECEIVER

Dead Deceiver

victoria houston

TYRUS
BOOKS

Published by
TYRUS BOOKS
1213 N. Sherman Ave. #306
Madison, WI 53704
www.tyrusbooks.com

This is a work of fiction.
Any similarities to people or places,
living or dead, is purely coincidental.

Library of Congress Cataloging-In-Publication Data has been applied for.

15 12 13 12 11 1 2 3 4 5 6 7 8 9 10

9781935562269 (hardcover)
9781935562610 (paperback)

It's a shallow life that doesn't give a person a few scars.

-*Garrison Keillor*

CHAPTER 1

Bracing herself on the open tailgate of her Jeep Liberty, Kathy Beltner jammed first one foot, then the other into the leather toeholds of her aluminum snowshoes. She bent to tighten the straps, then shook both feet to be sure the damn things would hold. God, how she hated it when—just as she hit a good stride—one would slip off. But these cost enough that they better stay on.

As she reached for her mitts, she glanced up at the sky. It was already after three, later than she liked, and overcast with plump puffs of snow lazing their way through the crisp air. Key ring in hand, she hit the button to lock the car, then tucked the keys into her fanny pack, adjusted the straps on her mitts and headed into the woods.

Hurrying along, she found the fresh snow light and easy going. The pale scrim of snowflakes that masked the trail was a wonder of silence with only a random swish of her snowshoes to be heard. She smiled to herself. An hour from now she would be in the hot tub, glass of red wine in hand, while Rob cooked dinner. Having a husband who loved to cook and two kids in college miles away was not a bad deal. Except for one miserable stepmother, life was good.

The very thought of Marian prompted Kathy to pick up her stride. No wonder she was out here today: she needed to work off the stress. And snowshoeing five miles at a brisk pace might just do it. On the other hand, Kathy cautioned herself, don't let dealing with that self-absorbed emotional midget get in the way of enjoying these lovely woods.

But it was tough to keep her mind off the situation. Marian was complaining again that the estate left by Kathy's late father was so small that Kathy should give her inheritance to Marian. Unbelievable.

Kathy tromped on, shoving snow-laden branches out of her way as if they were Marian herself. The shoving helped a little. She stopped to blow her nose and look around. The sky had grown darker, the snow so heavy now it was hard to see more than ten feet ahead. She had missed the trail, lost in brooding over Marian, and veered onto a deer trail by mistake.

But she was prepared. This wasn't the first time she'd missed the entrance to the south loop. Of course, the first time it had taken her three hours to find her way back to the parking lot. Since then, she always made sure to bring along a compass. She knew if she headed west, she was pretty sure she could find the west loop on the Merriman Trail System—and once she found that trail, she should be able to connect back to the south loop without losing too much time.

Her only regret was she would miss the lake—she loved the trail along the lake, with its wooden bridge and the point where she liked to pause and say a prayer in memory of her dad.

Checking the compass, she turned towards the west. The snow was so dense she was relieved she had not forgotten to wear her headlamp. Between the overcast sky and the snow, it would have been impossible to see more than a few feet ahead. She checked her watch: after four. Unzipping her fanny pack, she decided to call home and let Rob know … oops, darn. She'd left the cell phone in the car. Oh well, onward.

Bushwhacking through a stand of aspen, she glimpsed a bright light ahead. She headed towards it. A light meant a house, a barn, a garage—it meant someone was around. Someone who could tell her where she was exactly. Maybe ask them to give Rob a call and let him know she was running late.

As she neared the patch of light, the trees gave way and she found herself several hundred feet from a small wooden cabin. Two windows faced her, glowing from within. Attached to one corner of the building was a lantern illuminating a depression in the snow that had been a path winding towards the front door.

Somewhat out of proportion to the size of the cabin, which could not be more than eight hundred square feet, was a crow's nest jutting from the roof with glass windows on all four sides, almost like a deer stand.

That's innovative, thought Kathy, but I guess if you're going to build a cabin this far out in the woods, why not have it do double duty?

The light radiating from the lower windows made the little place looked so cozy, she breathed a sigh of relief as she started towards the cabin. She knew it was silly but when it got this dark and she was all by herself, she had a hard time sublimating her worry over wolves. Though no humans had been approached—yet—everyone in Loon Lake was aware that six packs patrolled the forests along the Merriam Trail. To re-phrase it: bear hunters no longer trained their dogs there.

Pausing to check her watch, Kathy had a sudden sense that she was no longer alone. She peered beyond a log pile to her right and caught sight of a tall, dark figure standing, watching her. "Excuse me," she said in a voice she hoped was loud enough to reach the man in the shadows, "how far is the road from here? Afraid I got off the trail and ..."

"You're on private land." The low, loud growl was not friendly.

"Well, I'm sorry but—I'm lost. I started out on the Merriam Trail, the south loop, and turned onto a deer trail by mistake. I didn't realize ...

"Who sent you?"

"Who sent me?" She half laughed as she spoke. "No one even knows I'm here."

As the man came towards her, the only sound was the soft swish of his boots through the snow. She strained to see his face but he wore a hooded sweatshirt under his parka, the hood pulled so far down over his eyes that even with the beam from her headlamp, all she could make out was a chin.

"Turn that thing off—that thing on your hat," he said, aiming a flashlight into her eyes.

"Sure, sorry about that," said Kathy, reaching for the On/ Off switch. She blinked in the harsh light from his torch, hoping he would return the favor. "If you'll just point me in the right direction? I'll get off your property right away. And I am sorry to have bothered you."

She widened her eyes in apology, her lips pressed tight in what she hoped was a charming grimace. As she waited for him to answer, disbelief tinged with confusion filled her eyes. He didn't answer. He raised his right hand. She had a split second to register the .357 magnum revolver: Her dad had owned one of those.

CHAPTER 2

Rob Beltner pulled the roasted chicken from the oven and jiggled one drumstick to be sure it was done. Perfect. He poured himself a second glass of wine and checked the time. Six thirty. Nearly two hours late. Boy oh boy, he hoped Kathy had remembered her headlamp this time.

After folding a sheet of aluminum foil into a tent, he tucked it over and around the chicken to keep it warm. A French baguette, sliced and spread with pats of garlic butter, rested on the counter—ready for warming the moment she walked in. The chopped romaine salad, already tossed and glistening with olive oil, reflected the flames from the candles on the kitchen table.

Rob blew out the candles, picked up the last section of the newspaper and, after re-arranging the kitchen chairs, settled in, feet up, to wait.

At eight o'clock, he called 911.

Lewellyn Ferris had just raised her fork with the first bite of buttery, flaky walleye when her cell phone rang. She checked the number, straightened up as she set her fork down and took the call. Sitting across from her at his dining room table, Paul Osborne watched with anxious eyes, hoping this wasn't an emergency that might ruin their evening. An evening that up until now had been off to an excellent start.

Fresh-caught walleye dipped in seasoned flour and lightly sautéed in butter was his dinner guest's favorite dish. Accompanying the golden portions were his own homemade coleslaw and cheesy mashed potatoes: the perfect meal for a cold winter's night.

Even the day had started well. Osborne's neighbor, Ray Pradt, had stopped in for his usual late morning cup of coffee only to surprise him with a Ziploc containing what had been a twenty-two inch walleye—filleted and ready for the skillet. "E-x-x-cel-l-l-ent morning for walking on water, Doc," said Ray, generous with syllables as usual. "Got two for me ... one for you ... and a couple for the good nuns." Neither of them commented on the fact that Ray's catch was double the legal limit.

Lew had added yet another pleasant surprise to Osborne's day by accepting without hesitation his offer to cook dinner. And dinner at his house meant, under normal circumstances, that she would spend the night. But well aware that the call to her cell phone would have been patched through by the night operator on the Loon Lake Police Department switchboard—and then only because there must be a serious incident of some sort—Osborne held his breath.

"Roger, you cannot ticket someone for a law that doesn't exist," said Lew, interrupting the caller in an exasperated tone as she rolled her eyes at Osborne. Her shoulders relaxed as she spoke, her right hand reaching for the fork. Shaking his head as he looked down at his own plate, Osborne repressed a grin. Roger had a knack for driving Lew nuts.

The eldest deputy on the Loon Lake police force, though the newest member and still learning, Roger had decided on law enforcement as a second career, thinking he could coast to retirement writing tickets along Main Street for over-parked tourists. No such luck. Lew kept him on the town streets pursuing over-served ice fishermen, hunters, snowmobilers and other miscreants—an annual motley assortment that needed policing through the winter months.

It was a motley assortment that was swelling in numbers thanks to the pending debut of Loon Lake's first ever International Ice Fishing Tournament. The tournament promised to bring in ice fishermen from fifteen countries plus vendors of food and equipment—not to mention spectators. Before the week was out, their little town was expected to swell from a population of 3,172 to nearly 10,000, with most of the visitors planning to stay until the end of February, which was a good two weeks away.

Already short-handed due to winter colds and flu bugs, both the police and the sheriff's department were depending on help from surrounding towns and counties. Meanwhile, since the hordes had begun to descend, Lew and her two officers had been working overtime.

"I don't care *where* he scattered the ashes," said Lew, continuing to sputter into her cell phone, "the fact remains there is no law against that ... Right, Roger. Please tell the property owners if they don't believe you, they can register their complaint with the police department in the morning. I'll take it up with the City Council. Now I'd like to finish my meal. Okay?"

Lew paused before repeating herself, "... yes, the City Council. It will require a new regulation ... I have no idea what they will do, Roger. But I will bring it up with the mayor in the morning. Tell those people exactly that and ask them to please, settle down. Okay?"

"Jeez Louise," said Lew, banging the cell phone onto the table. "I put in fourteen hours today and all I want to do right now is eat my dinner. Is that too much to ask?"

"What the heck is Roger up to?" asked Osborne.

Lew took two bites and closed her eyes before answering, "Ohmygosh, Doc, this … is … delicious." She wiped at her lips with a napkin, then said, "Seems that Myrtle Lund, who passed away last week, stated in her will that she wished to be cremated with her ashes scattered over the lake in front of that lovely home she and Dick owned before he died. The manager for St. Mary's Cemetery tried to make arrangements but the new owners didn't like the idea."

"Really," said Osborne, helping himself to more potatoes. "Wonder why? Doesn't sound harmful to me. As I recall, Myrtle had Dick's ashes scattered over the lake but that would have been before she moved into assisted living. Do the new owners realize she simply wanted to be with her late husband?"

"I don't know the whole story but apparently Ray Pradt assured the manager, Father John, *and* the Lund family that he would handle it."

"Uh-oh," said Osborne. "I imagine that since the cemetery gives Ray plenty of work digging graves when the guiding business is slow, he feels he has to do what he can to help."

"I understand that," said Lew. "But late night drive-by scatterings of cremated clients? That's a bit extreme, don't you think?"

Osborne chuckled as he scooped up a second helping of coleslaw and said, "Look at it from Ray's perspective. His grave digging business is way down due to the economy—not to mention the weather. Much cheaper to be cremated these days. No doubt he sees a financial opportunity in helping people with their ashes."

"I'm not going to argue the economics of the funeral business, Doc. Problem is Ray attempted to execute the scattering of poor Myrtle's ashes *after* the cemetery manager had been told by the property owners that it was not acceptable."

"Hmm," said Osborne, glancing out the kitchen window towards the garage and the floodlight illuminating the driveway. He gestured with his fork, "Look at that snow. I can't imagine that any ashes wouldn't have been covered within minutes. How on earth did he manage to get caught?"

"The couple who own the place spotted his headlights, found him parked down by their boathouse and called in on the 911 line. He might be at risk for trespassing," said Lew, spearing another portion of walleye.

"I wouldn't be so sure about that," said Osborne. "The Lund property abuts the public landing for that lake. In fact, there is a shared driveway. I know because it used to drive old man Lund crazy when people left their boat trailers blocking his way. Lew," said Osborne, putting down his fork and leaning forward on his elbows, "why do the new owners care so much about a few ashes? How about some basic kindness towards the bereaved family, for heaven's sake."

"I'm sure I'll hear all about it tomorrow," said Lew with a sigh of resignation. "Ray's argument, of course, will be that he meant well."

"He always 'means well,'" said Osborne, thinking of Ray's chronic violations of bag limits and fishing private water. The good news was that Ray tended to go over the limit by a half dozen or less—a pretty small number of fish, which ensured that any resulting fines would be affordable.

On the rare occasions that he got caught, Ray's excuse was always the same: the unlawful catch was intended for those "caring, hard-working nuns at St. Mary's who could not afford to attend Friday fish fry," as if religious intent could cancel the law.

But in the northwoods of Wisconsin, private water is private and bag limits are set in the same stone as the Ten Commandments: Not even the good Lord is allowed to violate those laws.

Lew's cell phone rang again. She answered saying, "For Crissakes, Roger—" Then she paused, listening, a frown crossing her brow before she said, "Oh, sorry, Sheriff. Yes, this is Chief Ferris. I thought you were one of my officers calling back … what is it? Where?"

Pushing her plate away, Lew got to her feet. "I'm on my way." Snapping the phone shut, she handed her plate to Osborne and said, "Doc, please, put it in the fridge. We'll nuke it when I'm back."

"What's up?" said Osborne as he helped her slip into her parka.

"Missing skier out on the Merriman Trial. Sheriff is shorthanded just like we are. I'm the only available officer. Doc, I'm sure I'll be back within an hour or so. One of the forest rangers is meeting me there with a couple snowmobiles. I can't imagine we won't find the skier shortly. Very likely she had an equipment failure and is walking out." She stood on her tiptoes to give him a swift kiss.

Watching Lew's squad car back around to leave his driveway, Osborne turned to the black lab sniffing around the dining room table, coveting the unfinished plates. "Not so fast, Mike. I'm hoping she'll be back—or it will be a long, cold night once again."

Grinning at the sound of his master's voice, the dog sat back on his haunches, eyes happy and tail thumping on the floor.

"Thanks for the offer, fella," said Osborne, "but I prefer you stay in your own bed."

CHAPTER 3

As she pulled into the parking lot at the trailhead, Lew saw three vehicles parked at a distance from one another: A black SUV, a maroon van, and a Forest Service truck with its tailgate down. Two snowmobiles had been unloaded from the truck and a figure bulked out in a dark green parka, padded gloves, and a white helmet with a Forest Service emblem was climbing onto the driver's seat of one of the sleds—an industrial-size snowmobile with a stretcher on runners attached.

Pulling her squad car alongside the truck, Lew gave a quick wave and parked. Reaching under the seat for her warmest pair of gloves, she popped the lever for the trunk and climbed out of the car. Wet, cold snow hit her in the face. Hurrying around to the trunk, she retrieved a snowmobile helmet and turned towards the rider on the approaching snowmobile. The rider raised her helmet shield as she spoke, "Chief Ferris, Ranger Lorene Manson. Appreciate you're giving me a hand."

Lew recognized the forest ranger, a broad-faced woman with reddened cheeks, strands of straw-colored hair plastered against her forehead and a dripping nose, which she wiped at with one finger of a heavily padded glove. Lorene Manson spent most of her time fining cross-country skiers who had not purchased trail passes. She did not look happy to be out this late.

"Happy to be of assistance, Lorene. You know where we're going?"

"Somewhat. The husband of the missing woman is keeping warm in his van over there. We'll take him with us since he knows the route his wife usually takes."

"Does he have a helmet?" said Lew.

"I brought two extra besides the one I'm wearing. I gave him one and strapped the other onto that stretcher back there along with some blankets. You all set?"

"Almost. Give me a minute to get familiar with this sled, will you?"

"Take your time, Chief. I'll have Mr. Beltner ride behind me. Man, this snow is not helping," said Lorene, pushing at the snow falling in her face as if she could make it go away.

As the ranger spoke, a tall, angular man in a bright red ski jacket of the type worn by cross-country skiers got out of the van, and paused to pull on the Forest Service helmet and adjust a small backpack he was wearing before striding over to the where the women were waiting. His helmet shield up, Lew could see dark, worried eyes. "Rob Beltner," he said, holding a hand out towards Lew. "It's my wife we're looking for."

"Chief Ferris with the Loon Lake Police," said Lew. "You called in the 911?"

"Yes, twenty minutes ago. She should have been home by four thirty." His voice cracked on the last two words.

"I'm assuming one of those two vehicles was driven by your wife?" Lew pointed a gloved finger towards the van and the SUV.

"The Honda CRV is Kathy's," said Beltner. "She always parks here, snowshoes the trail for an hour or two and returns to her car. It was locked when I got here. That's a good sign, maybe? That no one broke into the car? Her cell phone is there, too. My wife always forgets something. She tends to do that when she's in a rush."

"Now which trail does she ski?" said the ranger, motioning for Beltner to climb onto the seat behind her. As he did, Lew turned the ignition key on her sled, revved the throttle and tested the brakes. Then, letting her sled idle, she waited for Lorene to take the lead.

"She doesn't ski," said Beltner, shouting over the low rumble of the sleds, "she snowshoes and there is only one trail—that one." He pointed towards the rear of the parking lot.

"You holding on, Mr. Beltner?" asked Lorene with a tip of her head towards her passenger. "This may not be the smoothest ride."

"I'm ready," said Beltner, resting gloved hands on the ranger's waist, "just *please*—can we get going?" His words ended in a sob.

"Mr. Beltner—" said Lew.

"Rob."

"Okay, Rob," she said, adopting a reassuring tone. "The sheriff's department rescued a skier out here just last week. He'd broken the binding on one ski and was chilled but otherwise okay. It's a long walk if your equipment malfunctions back in on one of those loops. I'm pretty certain the worst that can happen to your wife is hypothermia."

"Or a broken leg," said Rob, his tone grim.

"Like I said—hypothermia." Lew reached over to pat him on the shoulder. "Aside from our concern right now, is your wife in good health?"

"Excellent health. She snowshoes five miles twice a week. That's how come I know she always takes the south trail to the lake."

The two snowmobiles charged onto the trail, snow billowing off into the darkness. The lead sled's strong headlight made it possible for them to maintain a good speed as they hurtled past the trunks and bare branches of oaks and maples guarding the snowshoe path.

Soon, as the forest morphed from hardwoods to evergreens, the trail closed in on them: snow-laden branches of balsam and spruce hung heavy overhead. Twice they had to skirt sagging limbs blocking the way.

Ten minutes down the trail, Lorene's headlight exposed a wooden railing. She stopped so quickly that Lew had to pull off to one side in order to avoid running into the stretcher.

"Sorry, Chief," said the ranger after jumping off her sled and running back towards Lew. She shoved her helmet shield up and leaned forward: "There's an access road used by loggers back in here. We should check it in case our person decided to take that route out."

"Right," said Lew, switching off the ignition on her sled. Leaning into the wind, Lorene tackled the drifts skirting the access road and Lew started after her, their boots crunching through over a foot of frozen layers hidden beneath the soft surface.

After a few yards, she looked back to see Rob Beltner, flashlight in hand, heading towards the wooden railing, which ran for a distance along a snow-covered boardwalk to end in at a ten-foot-long bridge over a burbling spring-fed stream. Lew knew the spot from years of fly fishing in the area—just as she knew a small lake lay beyond the bridge and that the springs kept the water flowing all winter long.

"Someone has been here within the last few hours," said Lorene, pointing to a series of depressions still discernible in spite of the new snowfall.

"Yep," said Lew, pausing to study the depressions. Definitly the tracks of someone's boots, not snowshoes. They seemed a little large for a woman—though Kathy Beltner would have had to remove her snowshoes in order to leave these tracks, and she was likely to be wearing an insulated boot. Of course, Lew and Lorene were both wearing heavy snowmobile boots that would leave large holes in the snow. Before Lew could speculate further, the depressions ended at a disappearing set of parallel tracks.

"Looks like an ATV to me—" Before Lorene could say more, a shout came from the direction of the boardwalk. They turned to see Rob Beltner staggering through the deep snowdrifts towards them.

"Blood," he gasped, pulling his helmet from his head. "I think I see blood in the snow along the bank by the bridge." As they followed him back towards the bridge, Lew's flashlight picked up more depressions, more boot prints in the snow. The tracks led down an incline and along the stream bank.

She looked up. Rob was hanging over the wooden rail and pointing at a snow bank on the opposite side. The creek, ignorant of human worry, bubbled merrily under the bridge, which cleared it by two feet and allowed the water to rush pell-mell into the lake, whereupon it disappeared under the ice.

As the beams from their flashlights raked the snow bank, Lew could barely make out a dark stain etching its way through the new snow. It appeared to start from a high point somewhere under the bridge to flow in a sharp diagonal down across the bank before disappearing into the lively water. One hour later and that stain would have been buried under fresh snow.

CHAPTER 4

"**R**ob, stop! You *must* stay on the bridge," said Lew, her voice fierce as she tried to keep Rob from scrambling down onto the snow-covered humps of swamp grass lining the stream.

"It's my wife, goddammit," said Rob, refusing to take direction as he leapt through the snow along the bank. He stumbled and pitched forward off balance—long enough for Lew to grab the back of his jacket and hold on. She pulled him down, hard.

"Please, Rob. I'm a police officer and this may be—" Lew looked up at the ranger watching them from the bridge, "Lorene, you come down here and stay with Mr. Beltner. Rob, you stay right where you are. You can watch from there."

Satisfied that the two would follow her instructions, Lew yanked off her helmet. After setting it to one side on the snowbank, she stepped into the rushing water and moved forward until, crouching, she could aim her flashlight under the bridge. Edging his way along the bank behind her, Lew could hear Rob's breath harsh in his chest.

She didn't like what she saw and paused before asking in a soft voice, "Was your wife wearing a red jacket with a white band across the shoulders?"

"Yes ..." Lew heard his boots hit the water behind her.

"Rob, stay where you are, please."

"Is she unconscious? Did she slip off the bridge?"

Before answering, Lew felt for a pulse on the woman's wrist—even though what she saw told her everything she needed to know. The beam of her flashlight followed the lines of the woman's body, which was folded in on itself and wedged into the space above the water line where the wooden bridge met the stream bank.

If it hadn't been for the slow seepage of blood from the entrance wound, Kathy Beltner might never have been found until summer. By that time the eagles and the ravens would have spirited much of her away, leaving only scraps of clothing and a skeleton for some hapless hiker to find on a lovely summer day.

On rare occasions, Lew hated her job. It is a heartbreak to ask a man to identify the woman he loves after a .357 Magnum has nearly obliterated her face.

Lew turned away from the sight of Kathy's corpse and spoke in a low tone. Rob was silent, dumbfounded. "I … what do I do?" he asked, raising his gloved hands in a gesture of helplessness.

"Not a thing right now," said Lew. "I have to get the coroner out here, get photos taken, get the EMTs to move her." She reached for her cellphone, then paused as Rob turned away, shoulders drooping.

"I just don't believe this," he said.

"I am so sorry but it is a crime scene and I have protocols—" Lew paused. She stepped back to let him by as she said in a soft whisper, "Rob, before I make this call … would you like to take her hand and say … 'goodbye' or …?"

Dropping to his knees, for a long moment Rob stared at his wife's body as if hoping, praying to see her breathe. Giving up, he pressed his cheek against the red jacket. He whispered words that Lew couldn't hear and then he cried, his body heaving with deep, harsh sobs that Lew understood too well.

The night she cradled the dead body of her only son, knifed in a bar fight when he was still a teenager, was etched moment by moment in her memory. No matter how fast she might find the person who had stolen Kathy Beltner from her family, no matter the   severity of the punishment—Rob's pain would never be lessened. He would never forget.

Leaving Rob to softly stroke his wife's still form, Lew waded a few feet back in the rippling stream and turned away, her cell phone out as she waited for the switchboard to patch her through to the coroner's home. "Evelyn," she said in brisk tone when the phone was answered, "Chief Ferris here. Put your husband on, please … *what?* When did that happen? Oh for Chrissake. All right. Will he be released tomorrow? Tell him to call in the minute he's alert.

"Jeez Louise," said Lew, hitting buttons on her cellphone again, "Doc? Sorry to call you like this."

CHAPTER 5

It wasn't until two minutes after ten that Osborne considered giving up hope that Lew would return. For her to be gone this long meant the situation involving the missing skier must be serious. He certainly hoped no one had died.

Fatality or not, he knew from experience that Lew would be determined to complete her paperwork. She hated leaving it for the next day. "Paperwork just piles up, Doc, and the next thing I know I have to spend a perfectly good afternoon when I could be in my garden or fishing the Prairie with you—doing the goddamn paperwork instead."

Osborne admired her persistence. He liked to think they shared that trait. Over his years of practicing dentistry, his perfectionism was unyielding: if the fit or feel of a gold filling or a fixed bridge were not flawless, he would work with the patient and the dental lab until it was.

He glanced at his watch for the umpteenth time: ten thirty. Okay, he gave up. But he did expect her to call and let him know she was okay. How many times had they had *that* discussion?

"You are the only woman I know who spends her working hours with a nine-millimeter weapon on her hip," he would remind Lew even as she grimaced, "so when you are on the job—I worry." And shortly after they had met, Officer Lewellyn Ferris had been promoted to Chief of the Loon Lake Police

Department, so she was "on the job" most of the time.

"But, Doc, you realize that means calling you every day?"

"So? Works for me." He did not add that the sound of her voice never failed to remind him that no matter his birthday, he was, at heart, a sixteen-year-old with a crush.

"Oh you!" And so they bantered, but she always called. Even if she had to wake him up.

Happy and content in spite of Lew's absence, Osborne set about getting ready for bed. Given they were both devotees of a good night's sleep he did not take it personally. Tucking her unfinished dinner, which he had covered with foil, into a Ziploc that would keep it moist, he set it in the refrigerator and glanced around the kitchen to be sure he had everything in order.

The dishes had been placed in the dishwasher and the frying pan washed and set in the rack to dry. The dog had been let out for the last time. Noting the near-zero temps outside and the Weather Channel's reports of increasing winds during the night, he decided to slip on the warmest of his flannel pajamas. That done, Osborne settled into his easy chair with the hardcover edition of *Trout Madness*, which Lew had given him for his birthday. Mike curled up on the rug next to the chair and with a heavy sigh rested his chin on his front paws.

Reading Robert Travers' essays on fly fishing the rivers and streams of Michigan's Upper Peninsula had become his favorite way to end an evening of solitude—almost but not quite as satisfying as a warm summer night of fly fishing with that local police chief who, having stayed on top her paperwork, treasured the hours when she could set her gun aside in favor of waders.

Osborne set the book on his lap and leaned back, eyes closed, to savor the wave of contentment that swept over him so often these days. He and Lew had fallen into a comfortable pattern of three or four nights together each week. He might kid her with the option of marriage—but only as a joke those evenings she hooked three rainbows and he got none. "You can catch and release those beauties," he would say, "but I refuse the release. I'm hooked and I'll stay hooked. Let's set a date."

Lew would greet his words with a grin but she was adamant. "Now, you know better than that, Doc. You know how much I love my farm—even if it is tiny and on a tiny little lake with tiny little bluegills. Too tiny for two."

"I know. But a guy can hope, can't he?" Lew would catch his eye with a smile and a shrug and make no more comment.

But if it was a pattern of togetherness they both found comfortable, it was also a pattern that left him liking *himself* better. Better than he ever had during his thirty-odd years of marriage to the late Mary Lee. He thought about that often. It seemed to have taken him forever to learn that there are people in your life with whom you're just … comfortable. They can stand next to you and not say anything, but you feel good. Just *comfortable*.

He knew three people like that: His youngest daughter, Erin. Ray Pradt, his next-door neighbor who might be thirty years younger but as talented as God when it came to fishing. And Lewellyn Ferris. How lucky can a guy be who—

Before he could finish that thought, the phone shrilled.

"Doc? Sorry to call so late like this," said Lew. He could hear a crackle through the phone line, which meant that she must be on her cell phone and at a distance from a cell tower. "I've got a homicide out here on the Merriman Trail and our trusty coroner is in the hospital."

"Pecore? In the hospital?" Cordless phone in hand, Osborne

jumped up from his chair and headed towards the bedroom.

"Yeah, seems he slipped on ice coming out of the Loon Lake Pub and may have a broken shoulder. Wonder how many martinis that took? How soon can you get here?"

"Give me time to get some clothes on and," Osborne checked his watch, "I'd say twenty minutes. Do we know the victim? Need an ID?"

"Kathy Beltner, Doc. Rob Beltner's wife. Cause of death appears to be a gunshot wound. Rob Beltner is here with myself and a ranger—no question the victim is his wife. But I can't move the body without an official sign-off on cause of death *and*," Lew sounded frustrated, "I'm hoping to heck you can rouse Ray to help with photos. I know it's late but I'm afraid the weather could screw up any evidence if—"

"I'll call him right now. Kathy Beltner, Lew? Gee, I hate to hear *that*. I know the family. Who on earth—"

"You know the trailhead, right, Doc?" She cut him off so fast, Osborne realized Rob Beltner must be standing nearby.

"Yes, I sure do. Will you be in the parking lot?"

"The forest service is sending someone to meet you in the lot at the trailhead. You'll likely find the EMTs there, too, but be sure the ranger brings you and Ray in first. Don't forget a snowmobile helmet—and, Doc, sorry about this."

"Please, Lew, not to worry. Be there ASAP." He set the phone down feeling both sad and elated. Sad for the stricken family, elated for himself. Working with Lew was more than just work.

CHAPTER 6

Osborne punched in his neighbor's phone number. "Yeah?" said a drowsy voice followed by a thud.

Osborne waited for the phone to be rescued then said, "Ray? It's Doc."

"Jeez, what time is it?"

Osborne spoke fast and did not wait for a response. "So I'll be over to pick you in about five minutes, okay?"

"Um, hold on a minute," said Ray. Osborne could hear bedcovers rustling in the background. "Any idea how long this might take? I'm s'posed to audition for that reality show at nine in the morning. Hate to miss that."

"Then I won't pick you up. Meet me at the Merriman Trail trailhead with your lights and camera. That way you can shoot what Lew needs and head straight home. She wouldn't ask you if—"

"I know," said Ray in a resigned tone. "I can use the dough anyway. See ya out there."

Osborne backed out of the garage and turned onto the town road. Pellets of snow flew straight into his windshield, stark white against an opaque blackness. To avoid vertigo, he forced his eyes to focus far ahead. His headlights, dimmed by spray from salt on the roads, did a poor job of illuminating the white streaked ribbon that passed for a road. Snow hiding the white lines that marked the shoulder forced him to slow down. This was no night to get stuck in a snow bank.

As he drove, he mused—as he always did when the Loon Lake Police Chief deputized him to fill in for their reliably errant coroner—on the unpredictability of life. Here he was driving to see a dead body in the middle of nowhere in the middle of the night in the middle of a snowstorm—and happy about it! Happy about lots of things.

A second career as a forensic odontologist? Learning to fly fish at his age—this old musky guy? Getting to spend time with a woman who loves the lakes and the rivers and the streams as much as he does? Who would have thought?

After all, just three years ago it was the worst of times.

Career-wise life had hit an all-time low. At his late wife's insistence he had sold his practice and retired from a profession he loved.

It was Mary Lee who had added it all up: their investment accounts, the escalating (exponentially) value of their lake home, the money he could make from the sale of his practice (exponential again) and the fact that both daughters were grown and self-supporting. As had happened more than once during their married life, Mary Lee had made a unilateral decision: "Paul, we are well off and it is high time we," (she really meant *I*), "enjoy the lifestyle I assumed we would have when I married you."

The next thing he knew she was planning trips to Europe, lobbying for a more luxurious house, scheduling dinner parties to entertain her friends and their husbands—and checking the stock market every few hours. Her fixation on their income got so out of hand that their financial advisor fired her. Or, as she said to her friends, "resigned due to his inability to engage with his clients."

Well aware that he was risking her ire (though he knew it would be difficult for her to fire *him*), Osborne had dragged his feet. Rather than read brochures on barge trips through French wine country or go along with their real estate broker to look at lake homes on the pricier Manitowish chain, he would escape in his fishing boat—leaving before breakfast and returning as late in the day as he could.

One evening when he was lingering in his favorite musky hole up on Third Lake—an attempt to hide out from yet another dinner party—he ran out of gas. His trusty Mercury 9.9 outboard just sputtered and died leaving Osborne marooned so far up the chain that it would take hours to row back.

Feeling more than a little frantic, he had waved at a passing fisherman who slowed, assessed the situation and was kind enough to offer him a tow. "Yep, I know your boat—you're Doc Osborne, aren't you? We're neighbors now, did ya know? Nice to meet ya, Doc." It was as formal an introduction as he would ever get to the man who was not only his new next-door neighbor but a man to whom Mary Lee had taken an instant dislike.

"I *abhor* that man," she would say every time she caught sight of Ray's battered blue pick-up. Osborne would turn away so she couldn't see the half smile on his face. He still offered prayers of gratitude to all the angels, the saints and the Holy Trinity that night when his gas hit empty.

Well, ninety percent of the time he gave thanks. The remaining ten percent was dedicated to cursing when Ray would tell a particularly offensive joke or hold Osborne hostage to a commentary peppered with vowels pulled out like chewing gum. Talents unappreciated by Osborne.

After the rescue that night, they had taken to hollering at one another from their respective lawn chairs, perched over the water on their neighboring docks. But soon they were sitting side by side on Ray's dock: highly advisable as topics soon took a turn towards the confidential. Osborne knew he had a good buddy when he discovered Ray to be as comfortable discussing life's adversities as he was debating the best lure for walleyes when the wind is out of the west.

He found it amusing—even satisfying in a juvenile way—that this friendship irritated the hell out of his wife: "I do not understand why you speak to that man. Just look!" And she would shake an angry finger at the "disgusting view of that house trailer," which she insisted ruined the vista from her expensive double-paned windows.

It was Ray who, when Mary Lee insisted Osborne get rid of his patient files, jumped at the chance to help him devise a secret hiding place in the garage. Like kids building a fort they had plotted each detail with care: first the wait for Mary Lee's weekly bridge game to take place in Minocqua, a good hour's drive each way plus a guaranteed four to five hours devoted to brunch, cards and gossip.

Then the hurried construction of a room they hoped to make impossible for a wife to find. Thanks to Ray hiding supplies in his truck, they got an early start and in one afternoon were able to erect a wall of plywood behind Osborne's stored pontoon and, behind that, install a door opening from the side of the garage into the attached shed where he cleaned fish. The shed was Osborne's sanctuary; Mary Lee wanted nothing to do with fish guts.

When they had finished, it was Ray, younger and stronger, who helped him move the three antique oak file cabinets from storage, each drawer packed with years of patient records—records of work that he was proud of, records of more than just teeth and gums, fillings and dentures.

"Each of these ..." said Osborne stepping back after the file cabinets were in place and opening a drawer to pull out a file only to pause in embarrassment, "... well, I look at one and I feel proud ... of what I've accomplished ... I guess." Ray had nodded. He understood.

"Mary Lee thinks I'm crazy to hold on to these and maybe I am but—"

"Doc, your wife saves family photos, doesn't she?"

"Of course," said Osborne.

"Well ... watching your face when you open one of those files, it's like you've a got a real person in your hand. It's like ... when I pick up one of my surface mud puppies, Doc ... I remember the night, the moon and the forty-eight inch monster I caught ... e-e-e-very moment of the ex-x-x ... perience."

"You are exactly right, Ray. These aren't just paper files—these are *my* memories."

Spurred on by the success of that venture and inspired by his neighbor's outlaw ways, Osborne opted to stage an act of open rebellion by maintaining his membership in the Wisconsin Dental Society. As expected, Mary Lee went ballistic: "Paul Osborne, if you think paying five hundred dollars for an annual membership in an organization of people you no longer have a good reason to see ..." She glowered.

When Osborne reported her response that evening on the dock, Ray had shrugged and grinned and egged him on.

Keeping that membership in the dental society was a charmed decision. It was not just that he was able to enjoy the camaraderie of the men and women, fellow professionals and colleagues— many of whom he'd known since dental school and several who had become good friends (and frequent fishing buddies) over the years—but the dental society's monthly seminars quickly became some of his most interesting hours.

Forensic odontology, a focus of several of the seminars, had intrigued Osborne. Having served in the military after graduating from dental school, he was grounded in the basics of dental forensics, which are based on the fact that teeth and dental restorations are the strongest elements in the human body and able to survive the destructive influences of fire and exposure to the elements.

Over the years that Osborne had practiced dentistry that fact had not changed: pathologists and medical examiners still rely on teeth and dental records to identify the dead. When the seminars turned to covering enhanced uses of dental DNA, Osborne was fascinated, taking notes as avidly as a student and buying all the study materials.

As entranced as he was by this new avocation, it was of little help when Mary Lee died unexpectedly from bronchitis that turned deadly in the midst of a winter blizzard. She left behind a dangerous void. While she had never hesitated to remind him of all the ways in which he had not quite measured up as a husband, her fussing had given his life structure. When he lost her, he lost a world made safe by how she defined their days.

That was not a good year: No longer restrained by the pressures of a fulltime dental practice, no longer kept in line by his wife. No longer places to go or things to do.

Too much loss in too short a time led to too many shots of Bushmills.

Studying for the seminars forced some sobriety. That, plus a determination not to miss six thirty Mass each weekday, meant his mornings were sober if heavy-headed. But by noon he would be lost. Six months into killing himself, his daughters took over with an intervention that shook him hard: "Dad, do you want to see your grandchildren grow up? *Do you?*"

Rehab followed.

When he had returned from Hazelden, chastened and shaky, it was Ray who watched and waited for the right time to make a move. It was after a good day together in Osborne's Alumacraft (three walleyes over twenty inches each!) that he persuaded the recovering retired dentist to attend his group ("just this once, Doc") in the room behind the door with the coffee pot.

It was an evening as redemptive as the fishing. And so it was that Osborne and Ray made it a weekly habit: an afternoon of fishing in Doc's boat followed by an early dinner of sautéed catch at Ray's trailer and a drive to town for an evening session behind that door with the coffee pot.

Nearing the intersection where he would turn left towards the Merriman Trail, Osborne smiled. Life had its twists and turns, all right, but how could he have anticipated that an uncharacteristic urge to clean his garage would have led to a new career—and the chance to work with the woman with the dark, honest eyes and easy grin. He was a lucky guy.

It had been a Saturday mid-April two years ago, a morning so warm that in spite of the lake breeze he was able to keep the garage doors open while he swept up dead leaves and mounds of dirt left over from winter parking. That accomplished, he opted to organize his fishing gear.

After working through four tackle boxes, he checked each of his seventeen spinning rods to see which ones needed new line. Then a short break to fortify himself with an egg salad sandwich before returning to the garage and a jumble of cross-country ski equipment. That done, he saw other stuff that needed sorting.

He was restacking the eight plastic tubs holding Mary Lee's holiday ornaments when he discovered a rusty old gym locker hidden behind the tubs. Inside were three empty canvas gun cases and a bamboo fly rod that he vaguely remembered purchasing. It had never been used. On an upper shelf was a small box holding a reel loaded with fly line and two tiny plastic containers of trout flies on which someone had scrawled in black marker: "Woolly Buggers, Size 12."

Ah, thought Osborne, the trout flies must have been tied and given to him by a patient. Sitting down on a nearby bench, he examined the trout flies. He couldn't imagine how else these boxes had come his way. Had he bargained for them? Often over the years, when patients were down on their luck, he would barter for venison chops or fresh-caught fish. Had he done that with these?

Osborne sat there, tipping the boxes of trout flies this way and that. The trout flies were colorful, exquisite. Like the fly rod, which had not been cheap, they had been acquired before his late wife caught on to his budding interest in a new sport. That he knew because he had a vivid memory of Mary Lee putting her foot down: "Paul, you have enough fishing equipment. I refuse to let you spend another dime of our money—"

Later that same day he had driven to town and shown the fly rod to the owner of Ralph's Sporting Goods whom he knew to be an avid fly fisherman. The rod was a good one and Ralph was willing to take it on consignment but he encouraged Osborne to give fly fishing a try first.

"Doc, if you were interested once, who knows—you might like it. Spin fishing keeps you on the water but fly fishing takes you *into* the water. A very different experience. I know you love the outdoors and no doubt you own some waders—"

"Okay, okay, you don't have to twist my arm, Ralph," said Osborne, "but how do I get started? I've never cast a fly rod in my life."

"Tell you what, Doc. I know a real good instructor who can show you a few basics—help you decide if it's something you want to do ..."

And so he had agreed to let Ralph book him "half day" for a hundred bucks with a guy named "Lou." Ralph would make money on the booking, of course, but Osborne didn't mind. He had nothing better to do and why not give the rod and those trout flies a try?

Turned out to be the best hundred bucks he'd spent in years: "Lou" turned out to be "Lew"—a police officer moonlighting as a fly fishing instructor. Nor was "Lew" a guy. And as Osborne learned to cast a fly rod, Officer Lewellyn Ferris, on getting to know her student, was introduced to the concept of forensic odontology.

This was a trade that benefited both of them when, weeks later, the Loon Lake coroner was on one of his benders (alleged as always by his wife to be a "last minute vacation") just as an individual passed away under circumstances that required a signed death certificate before the family could deal with the remains. A certain police officer knew just whom to call.

"Doc," Lew had said when she called him the first time, "Pecore is hopeless around booze but there is nothing the department can do. He is appointed town coroner by the mayor and—since the jabone is married to the mayor's wife's sister—he's home free. We have to deal with him."

"Isn't that too bad," said Dr. Paul Osborne, managing to keep his tone serious even as he was delighted to be deputized to work with her. That occasion was soon followed by others, including the opportunity to ID crime victims.

When the current chief of police retired, Lewellyn Ferris was promoted to his position. Not only did this enhance her authority to deputize whomever she might need but Osborne's skills in dental forensics gave her leverage—and a direct benefit to her budget—as she could loan him out to the Wausau Crime Lab, which could not afford a full-time odontologist.

So it was that Dr. Paul Osborne found himself once again in a position to barter his dental skills: The Loon Lake Police Department could pay for his time or their Chief of Police could continue his fly fishing instructions in the trout stream—at no cost.

Talk about a no-brainer!

CHAPTER 7

"Hey, Doc, I hear the Chief got you out of bed, too, huh?"
"Almost—I was in my PJs."

The face grinning into the open window of Osborne's car belonged to Terry Donovan, the younger of Lew Ferris's two full-time officers. "Say," he said without waiting for Osborne to answer, "I picked up a four-wheeler from the sheriff's garage and dropped it off at the access road that runs up to the trails. Only way we can get back in there with our equipment. I've got Ray staying warm in my car here and thought I'd drive both you fellas back there. But I want you to leave your cars here at the trailhead."

"Do I need a helmet?" asked Osborne, reaching for the black bag in which he carried his notebook, blank death certificates and medical instruments. He peered through the window towards Terry's squad car where Ray was sitting. Osborne noticed he was wearing a helmet-like ski cap of the type worn by cross-country racers. Odd.

"Nah, you'll be fine. But speaking of helmets, what's with Ray? Last time I saw him he was wearing more lights than a Christmas tree. Tonight he looks, well, normal."

"No trout hat, huh?" Osborne was surprised, too.

Ray's hat was ubiquitous. Some people swore he slept in it. Even Osborne rarely saw him without the old leather aviator cap resting on his head, the furred flaps pulled down over his ears against the winter wind. Perched on top and hard to miss was a fourteen-inch stuffed brook trout. Draped across the breast of the fish was a double string of multi-colored blinking LED lights.

"Maybe he's trying to avoid hat hair," said Osborne. "He's auditioning for a TV show in the morning."

"No wonder he's so serious. Seems a little out of sorts, Doc. Got everything," said Terry, checking his watch as Osborne locked his car. "Sorry, but we gotta hurry. I gave the EMTs directions to that access road and I don't want them going in ahead of us."

"I'm set." Climbing into the back seat of the cruiser, Osborne looked over at Ray who was sitting with a camera case on his lap. Not only was he hatless but his beard looked recently trimmed. Then it dawned on Osborne: he'd bet anything Ray thought the local TV news crews might cover the story tonight. Any publicity is great publicity—and Ray was determined to land the role on ICE MEN.

"How did you get here so fast?" said Osborne, "Last we talked you were just getting out of bed."

"Took the back way on Jack Pine Drive," said his neighbor. "You know that shortcut, don't you?"

"I would not drive it in *this* weather. Hard enough to see on the main highway." Even as Osborne spoke he remembered that Ray had the eyes of a great horned owl: he could find his way anywhere—even in the dark.

Ray Pradt's quirky talents were a frequent subject of discussion by the early morning McDonald's coffee crowd—the daily gathering of old guys who would chew over the *Loon Lake Daily News'* police report to see if any of their relatives—or wives' relatives— were listed. This might be followed by speculation as to where one of their missing buddies was fishing that morning. Since not a one

of them ever told the truth as to where they put their boat in—the latter was an enjoyable waste of time.

When those subjects had been exhausted, they would turn to local gossip. On average about once a week—and assuming he was not present—that would include an update on the whereabouts and legal status of Ray Pradt.

Any recent misdemeanors? The guy might be on the straight and narrow when it came to booze but he had a weakness for mood enhancement induced by locally grown cannabis. One thing they were sure of: if anyone could find locally grown cannabis, it would be that rascal. At least he was wise enough not to grow it himself, as that was a sure ticket to jail time.

Then there was the tantalizing question of Ray's sex life. It wasn't that Ray had a weakness for women so much as the other way around. Of course it didn't help that he gave his girl-friends nicknames like Snowflake, Tornado and Firecracker. The McDonald's crew never could figure out what ladies found so attractive in a guy who wore a fish on his head. Shouldn't that be warning enough?

Lately, however, the coffee talk had been admiring: The Loon Lake Chamber of Commerce Annual Calendar had just been published and was arriving on doorsteps courtesy of the local Lions Club. Along with dates of local fishing events, church socials and holidays, each page featured eight-by-ten photos of outdoor photography captured by the coffee crowd's youngest member.

"Yep," Dick Zwolanek had said with a grudging shake of his head, "guy might be irritating as hell but he sure can shoot a sunset."

"He's okay," said Bert Kadubek, "I like Ansel Adams myself. Black and white beats color for me." Known as "the answer man" behind his back, the McDonald's crowd suffered Bert's presence in spite of his pronouncements.

"Sour grapes, Bert?" Osborne had said.

"Now, Doc," said Bert, backpedaling, "I thought he did a nice job with that photo of the newborn fawn hiding under the ferns—all those shades of green. Timed the light just right—probably has a real good light meter."

"My favorite's the snapping turtle," said Herm Dickson, butting in to demonstrate with a swoop of his arm that knocked over Bert's coffee. "That sucker looks like he's coming right at you. Shooom! Jumps right off the page."

"It's a zoom lens, Herm," said Bert, implying Herm was an idiot and he, Bert, could be just as good a photographer if he had the right equipment.

"Then why don't you goddamn do it?" Osborne wanted to say but didn't. You look worse arguing with Bert Kadubek than if you just roll your eyes.

But if Ray excelled at his outdoor photography—thanks to years of making a buck wherever, whenever and however he could (the Lions Club paid him five hundred bucks for all twelve photos)—he was equally good at shooting crime scenes. Significantly better than Pecore, whose eyes were often bloodshot, if not fogged over.

After the second time that Ray and Osborne were deputized to cover for Pecore, Osborne had joked to his neighbor that they had somehow managed to morph into a strange but effective 'dynamic duo.'

Lew agreed on that score: she got accurate reports from Osborne, which were respected both by the local pathologist as well as the Wausau Crime Lab. And she got excellent quality in the color and black and white photos from Ray's cameras. Plus, he was agile and able to shoot from the angles needed. More than once his photos had exposed surprises the eye couldn't catch at a crime scene.

The cruiser turned onto the access road, a narrow lane used by loggers. Enough activity had been taking place in recent months that random plowings by the loggers kept it passable. Terry parked next to the largest ATV that Osborne had ever seen.

"What the heck *is* this?" said Osborne, walking around the vehicle while Ray pulled an armload of tripods, lights and a battery pack from the trunk of the police cruiser. The ATV held four seats plus a small rear storage area. The seats and the storage were protected with side nets. Not as wide as a car, the ATV would be able to travel the snowmobile, ski and snowshoe trails easily. The fat, grooved tires might mess up the groomed trails but that was the least of worries if a life was at risk.

"Pretty cool, huh," said Terry. "The sheriff's office got the county to approve this four-wheeler—it's a Polaris Ranger RXR4—because of all the snowmobile crashes last year. Tough to get to those locations any other way. You sure can't drive a car down a snowmobile trail. You have an accident victim who needs to be airlifted to a hospital? You are flat out of luck with a two-seater snowmobile. This ATV can scramble up a snow bank like you wouldn't believe."

As he spoke, a large white ambulance with the St. Mary's Hospital logo on the sides pulled up behind the cruiser. Osborne recognized Mike Wittenberg at the wheel and was relieved. Mike was an experienced EMT who had assisted the Loon Lake Police more than once with homicide victims. He knew the drill.

"Dr. Osborne, good to see you as always," said Mike, opening his door and climbing out. "Chief Ferris said you have a possible homicide victim so I've got a fella following us with a three-wheeler in the back of his truck. My colleague, Jeanine here, and myself should be able to retrieve the body—"

"Hey, Mike," said Terry, walking over to the ambulance,

"do you mind moving your vehicle over to this side, please? Chief Ferris found some tracks leading from this area to where the victim was found. We don't want anyone walking over those."

"Tracks? What kind of tracks? Where?" said Ray. He had just set his camera bag and other gear in the back of the Polaris. Now he reached over for the camera bag and unzipped it.

"This way," said Terry. "Chief Ferris told me to have you get some photos before we meet up with her. She's worried this snow will cover 'em up."

Ray followed Terry ten feet beyond the ATV and watched as the officer knelt to brush away the fresh snow and expose a crisp layer beneath. "Right here," said Terry, pointing and aiming the beam of a flashlight. "You can see where that mist we got a couple hours ago froze so you can still make out … there … boot prints! Like someone parked along here, then got out of their vehicle and headed on foot towards the trail."

"And the trail is right back behind those balsams, isn't it," said Ray, lifting his head to look in the direction of the trees. "Yeah, this is good. The mist freezing like that is a bonus."

"Need more light?" asked Osborne, "I can bring over some of those tripods if you need 'em."

"Nope. Flash works fine." Camera whirring, Ray captured a quick series of photos, checked the results and nodded to Terry—"got it good."

"Okay, let's get going here," said Terry turning back towards the ATV, "Mike, you want to follow my tracks in when you're ready? Stay right on 'em, okay?"

As Terry was talking, the truck that Mike had been waiting for pulled up behind the ambulance. The driver hopped out and ran to the rear, dropped the tailgate and started to unload a small three-wheel ATV.

"We'll wait for them," said Terry to Osborne and Ray. The

three watched in silence as Mike and the driver worked to hitch a toboggan to the back of the second ATV. Aside from their bustling noises, the only sound to be heard was the "shush" of the falling snow. In less than five minutes, they were ready.

"Listen up, everyone," said Terry, shouting over the low roar of the ATVs. "Before we go in I want you to watch for two things. First, I will keep to one side of the trail so as not to run over any boot prints. So stay right behind me, please. When we get to the site where Chief Ferris is waiting, we will take direction from her on where to park.

"Doc, Ray, Mike—I know you know this but just a reminder that this is a potential crime scene so it is critical that we have just one route in and the same route out. Under no circumstances does anyone walk outside that route or go in any other direction unless you have permission. Everyone straight on that?"

All heads nodded as Mike said, "Got it—no need to worry."

CHAPTER 8

Just beyond the snow blowing into their faces, Osborne was able to make out the headlights of two snowmobiles parked less than a hundred yards down the trail. Terry slowed as they neared and the strong beam from their ATV picked up Lew's black parka as she walked towards them with a wave.

"Over there," she shouted, a gloved finger signaling to a spot on the left side of the trail just before it curved.

From where he sat, Osborne could see that the sleds ridden by Lew and the forest ranger had been positioned so that their headlights illuminated the dark outline of a handrail running along the top of a snow-covered wooden bridge just ahead. Under the bridge flowed a ribbon of open water no more than four feet wide. Just above the burbling water and tucked under the right side of the bridge he saw what looked like a small bundle the color of raspberries.

After waiting to be sure Terry would give Ray a hand unloading his equipment, Osborne grabbed his flashlight and hurried over to Lew. "Sorry to keep you waiting, Chief," he said.

"Hey, that's okay, Doc," said Lew. "It hasn't been that long and I'm just relieved I could get you and Ray out here. Damn that Pecore—though I know you two will do a better job anyway. Ready to follow me down?"

Without waiting for an answer, she started along a path leading down the snow bank towards the bridge. The stream running beneath the bridge was quite shallow, only a few inches deep. Once there, Osborne knelt and sat back on his heels to study the scene in front of him.

The victim's red ski jacket had been pulled down over her bent knees and tightened. His first impression was of a small child lying on its side, legs tucked up to take a nap—as innocent as one of his grandchildren. The thought sparked a tremor in his heart, worry over what he would learn next.

In life Kathy Beltner had been a small-boned, slender woman no more than five feet six inches tall. Death diminished her: she seemed tiny. Studying what was left of her face, he couldn't help but recall her cheery smile and lively ways. She had always impressed him as an exuberant young wife and mother. So much life gone. A face destroyed. Teeth missing.

This is what can happen to Lewellyn, thought Osborne, an unreasonable panic flooding his gut. One bullet can do this! Think of all the times she is called out on domestic disturbances where people have been drinking and guns are so easily accessed. Think of the vagrants high on drugs or alcohol—with a gun in their crummy car.

One solitary bullet slammed the life out of Kathy Beltner. That is all it would take to kill or maim Lewellyn Ferris. He would rather die himself than lose her.

Closing his eyes for a moment, he took a deep breath, then exhaled. Hey, stop thinking this way, he told himself. You have work to do, calm down.

Osborne dropped his head to say a sad, silent prayer then reached over to set his mitts on the snow beside his medical bag. He pulled on a pair of Nitrile gloves.

"You okay, Doc?" Lew laid a hand on his shoulder.

Osborne raised his head and checked to see where Rob Beltner was. Good, he was up on the trail and talking to the ranger. Out of earshot.

"This is not an easy one, Lew. I knew this woman. Rob, Kathy, their daughters—they were patients of mine. How's Rob taking it? Or is that a stupid question?"

"I don't know that it's hit him yet. You know how it is. People are so stunned the emotions come later."

"Is he a suspect?"

"Has to be. But do I really think he shot his wife? No."

"Is it okay for me to—" Osborne indicated with both hands that he was ready to approach the body.

"Please," said Lew. "My feet are starting to freeze and this snow is covering whatever evidence we might have had so work as fast as you can."

Leaning forward, he reached the zipper on the red jacket, managed to unzip it and gently prod past the knees, disturbing the body as little as possible. Beneath the jacket was a black fleece vest and under that a turtleneck of some soft fabric. Starting at the waist, he slipped his hand under the turtleneck and let his fingers slide up along the ribcage to the armpit. The victim's arms, which were folded against the chest, were not yet stiff with rigor.

Noting the condition of the armpit, Osborne pulled his hand down and away. With fingers as gentle as if swaddling a baby, he zipped the jacket shut over the knees so that Kathy Beltner appeared exactly as she had before his exam. Osborne turned his head to one side.

"Slight warmth in the armpit," he said and reached into his medical bag. Using two instruments, he nudged first the head, then what remained of the jaw. Both moved.

Osborne replaced the instruments, grabbed his mitts and stood up. "Given the warmth in the armpit and the lack of rigor in the neck and the jaw, I would guess she was shot within the last three hours. But," he raised a finger as if instructing himself, "with the amount of clothing the victim is wearing—and the temperature out here—that is a wild guess. Cold can delay the onset of rigor mortis by hours so you have many, many variables here, Chief."

"Thank you, Doc," said Lew. "Ray," she waved at the figure waiting by the ATV, his arms loaded with tripods and lights. "Your turn. Let me know what I can do to help. Oh, and Doc, the ranger standing over there with Rob Beltner is Lorene Manson. She knows you need time with him so don't hesitate."

As Ray scrambled down the path along the snow bank towards the bridge, Osborne stepped to the side to keep out of his way, taking care to disturb the snow on both sides as little as possible.

"Say, Chief," said Ray as he neared Lew, "I saw those boot prints back by the access road. Got good shots of them walking away and returning. I see more in this area but we have enough close-ups. How 'bout I shoot from a distance to show the range of activity around here. Need more than that?"

"Problem is, there's no sign of Mrs. Beltner's snowshoes," said Lew. "I was hoping you could take the time to search for them. Might give us some idea where she met up with the person who killed her because there is no evidence that she was shot anywhere around here. No blood spatter, nothing. And if anyone can find where it happened, it's you, Ray."

"Yikes," said Ray, "on a night like this that could take a while. It's not the dark, Chief, it's the snow that's covering everything— I'd be better off searching in the daylight."

"Well, just so you're in my office first thing in the morning. Got a call from Roger about you scattering someone's ashes on private property without permission. You and I need to get that matter resolved—"

"I know, I know and I'm sorry about that but I didn't do anything wrong." Ray set his tripods down and, hands on his hips, said in an exasperated tone, "I tried … to explain to those people that 'wildcat … scatterings' … are … legal. It's a new and accepted practice in the burial business."

"A wildcat *what*?" Lew sounded incredulous. "But, hey, I don't have time for this now. In the morning."

"Say … ah … Chief, I have a kinda life changing m-e-e-e-eting at nine?" said Ray, wheedling with raised eyebrows. He waited.

"Yes, you do. In my office. It likely affects if I am able to deputize you again … ever."

Ray said in a chagrined tone: "I have an audition for that reality show … if you're late, you don't get another chance. The producers only got two days to do over a hundred people …"

Lew hesitated a long minute then gave in. "All right but immediately afterwards, Ray. My office. I'm sorry but this ashes issue could involve the Mayor and the City Council. That was the Wheedon College president whose land you trespassed on.

"Promise me that following our meeting you'll head back out here. Okay? Terry will cordon off the entire trail and the access road as we leave here tonight. No one will be allowed in until you have covered the territory."

"That works, Chief. That works great—and I promise I will search every inch of this place—north, south, east and west," said Ray, waving his arms to include the universe.

CHAPTER 9

Back on the trail, Osborne walked to a spot about twenty feet from the west end of the bridge where Rob Beltner was standing with the forest ranger. Both were quietly watching Ray as he set up his tripods along the snow bank near the bridge. Figuring that for Rob, watching Ray shoot photos was kind of like watching his house burn, Osborne thought it wise to divert his attention.

"Hello, Rob," said Osborne, trying for the low, reassuring voice he had perfected for calming patients anxious over pending root canals. He reached to shake the man's hand saying, "I believe Chief Ferris told you that I would be standing in as acting coroner due to Mr. Pecore's accident?"

"Yes, she did, Dr. Osborne," said Rob, "not sure what you need from me, though. I'll do my best."

"What you can't answer tonight we can take care of in the morning, but it's pretty boilerplate and maybe will take us less than half an hour at the most."

Looking over at the ranger, Osborne extended his hand again and said, "Lorene, we haven't met. I'm Dr. Paul Osborne. Don't know if Chief Ferris mentioned I would be filling in for Mr. Pecore?"

"Lorene Manson, Dr. Osborne," said the forest ranger. "Yes, Chief Ferris told me she was lucky to be able to bring you in on this tonight. I know you need to complete some paperwork so let me give you two some privacy." She walked over to join Lew, who was deep in conversation with the EMTs.

"This way, Rob," said Osborne, motioning for Rob to follow him over to the large ATV, "let's take a seat here."

They settled into the front of the four-wheeler and Osborne pulled a clipboard from his medical bag. Rob answered his questions in a voice that grew more clipped with each query. When Osborne had to ask for the names and addresses of Kathy's parents, Osborne could see that the poor guy was barely holding it together. "That's enough for now," said Osborne, slipping the clipboard back into his bag.

"Dr. Osborne," said Rob, his eyes full of pain, "what do I do now? What the hell do I do now? How do I tell our children? Oh, my God," he said, and wept.

Osborne put an arm around his shoulders. He had no idea how to answer.

Two years earlier, after the trauma team had taken Mary Lee off life support at three a.m. that winter morning, he had asked himself the same question: What the hell do I do now?

He had been fortunate not to be alone. In spite of knowing that Mary Lee Osborne was the "anonymous party" lodging complaints with the town board in hopes of forcing him off his property, Ray Pradt had not hesitated for an instant when he got Osborne's call.

"It's my wife, Ray," Osborne had said in a voice quivering with panic. "She's having trouble breathing and the fever has spiked. I've got to get her to the hospital but the ambulance can't—" That was all Osborne had to say.

Though it was after midnight at the height of a raging blizzard with sub-zero temps and winds gusting forty miles an hour, Ray had stopped him before he could say more. "It'll take me five to bolt the plow on the truck. Wrap her up real warm. Be sure to cover her face and I'll be right there, Doc. You call the hospital and tell 'em we're on our way."

He had waited with Osborne while the emergency team worked. He was still there when Osborne got the news. Even as Osborne sat silent and stunned for a good half hour, gathering the strength to call his daughters—Ray stayed with him. Quiet. Ready to help in any way he could.

"Do you have a close friend we can reach by cell phone? Someone who might be able to help you out tonight?" said Osborne. "I'll make the call for you."

Rob was silent for a few beats then said, "Yes, I do know someone I would like to call. One of my colleagues in our engineering office. He and his wife are close friends of ours ... I think I can make that call." Looking down, he patted his jacket pockets. "Looks like I left my cell phone in my car."

Peering over Rob's shoulder, Osborne noticed that the EMTs had begun their preparations to move the body. This he really did not want Rob to see.

"You are welcome to use mine," said Osborne, handing over his cell phone, "but I suggest you stand close to the lake. You're likely to get better reception."

Rob climbed out of the ATV and walked across the trail to stand on the bank of the small lake. As he placed the call to his friend, Osborne got out of the ATV and walked onto the bridge. He looked out over the ice towards the distant shore then turned to follow the sound of open water noisy in the night air.

The lake was to the south of the bridge and its water spilled under the bridge to flow north, up and into the swamp. As he watched the current, it dawned on Osborne that the killer may have miscalculated when he was deciding where to hide his victim.

Looking around to find Lew, he saw her observing the EMTs as they slipped protective bags over Kathy Beltner's hands in order to preserve any debris under her fingernails that might indicate a struggle. Next they lifted the body with care and laid it on white sheets, which they folded over and around. Once they had strapped it onto the emergency toboggan, Osborne said, "Chief, do you have a minute?" He waved for her to join him.

"Be right there," she said as she climbed up the snow bank and walked his way. "I'm pooped, Doc. Ray's got all the photos I need so we can head back shortly. How you doing?"

"I'm fine but I think I know why we found our victim tucked under here."

"Because whoever it is thought they could hide the body under the lake ice only to discover it's so shallow along the shoreline that there was no way they could hide it there?" asked Lew.

"I don't think they realized that the stream *starts* at the lake and runs north into the swamp. I'll bet you anything they expected the water to be run under the bridge and *out into the lake*—strong enough to carry a body out, even if it took a while."

"You may be right, Doc. Ray and I were just saying it appears that some tools were carried in here, too. An axe and a saw at least."

"No ice auger?"

"Not that we can see."

"In that case, we're not looking for an ice fisherman who might have thought to drill a hole ten or twenty feet out from shore and drop the body into the lake ..."

"Or someone who didn't want to risk being seen by skiers out here. Quite a few folks cross-country ski in the dark these days—especially these trails because they are so level and they run around this lake.

"Doc, Ray said you two are parked in the lot at the trailhead so I am going to have Terry drive you two out the snowshoe trail here so he can cordon it off at the trailhead. I've told Rob that he can drive his car but he has to leave his wife's in the parking lot until I can get the Wausau boys up to take a good look at it."

She shook her head, "I just can't figure out how Kathy Beltner got down here since we don't see any sign of someone snowshoeing in to this area. At this point it appears that she was carried in by the individual who walked in from the access road—but how did she get *there*? We have boot prints but no sign of snowshoes."

As she spoke, Ray walked over to the ATV with his gear and set it down. "All set, Chief, I'll load these into the computer tonight and send them your way."

"Ray, I'm trying to figure out one thing," said Lew, and repeated her mystification over the lack of snowshoe tracks. "I know it's late but will you keep an eye out in case you see something as you drive back with Terry?"

Minutes later as Terry maneuvered the ATV down the trail through the overhanging branches loaded with fresh snow, Ray raised a hand for him to stop. "Hold on, let me check something." He got out of the ATV and walked along the trail a few feet, then came back. "Nothing, just a deer trail is all."

As he got back into the ATV, Osborne asked Terry, "how much snow have we gotten anyway?"

"I was told it's been falling at the rate of two inches an hour," said Terry.

"So between four this afternoon and right now, we've gotten anywhere from ten to sixteen inches of new snow?"

"Something like that."

"That's a bitch," said Ray. "Only saving grace might be that precip we got earlier. If that stays frozen, I might be able to scout tomorrow in the daylight."

"I know Lew is hoping you'll find the snowshoes. Locating where they were dropped might tell us more about what happened out here."

"Unless the killer kept them—as a trophy."

Osborne stared at Ray as the ATV bounced along the trail. "That's an unpleasant thought."

As Osborne gazed at her across the kitchen table, Lew wolfed down the rest of her dinner. It was past two in the morning and he had been pleasantly surprised when she said she would follow him home: "I have to, Doc, I left all my clothes for tomorrow at your place—oh, it *is* tomorrow. Oh well."

Soon after they slipped into bed. Osborne was careful to take his side, knowing she had to be exhausted. He turned out the light on bed table beside him. Outdoors, the snow had finally stopped. A haze of moonlight lit the room.

Lew moved against him in the dark.

"Are you sure?" he said.

"Doc," her voice was soft, "it's one way to remind ourselves that every minute counts."

CHAPTER 10

Sitting at the conference table in front of the west windows in Lew's office, Osborne sipped from his coffee mug as he checked through his notes from the night before. He wanted to be sure he had covered everything that he had observed from arriving at the trailhead to leaving three hours later.

This afternoon, he and Lew would compare notes. It wasn't unusual for each of them to see or hear different things. More than once observations that seemed insignificant at the time grew in importance as an investigation progressed.

Setting aside his notebook, he opened the folder holding the death certificate for Kathy Beltner, then checked his watch and considered whether or not to call Rob. Osborne needed Rob to find his wife's birth certificate in order to confirm the name of the hospital where she had been born. It was shortly after nine and while it might be early to call, Osborne doubted the poor guy had slept much anyway. Sympathy for the younger man swept over Osborne: he knew too well that for Rob Beltner, life would never be the same. For his two children, news of their mother's death must still seem like a bad dream.

"More coffee, Doc?" asked Lew, glancing over from where she sat at her desk working on the computer.

"Sure. I'll give Rob Beltner a call in a minute. This death certificate is almost complete—then I'll get out of your hair." After handing Lew his mug, he scanned the document one last time, making a mental note to put the name and address of the hospital where he had been born somewhere easy for his daughters to find when it was his turn to go—naturally or otherwise.

"You are *not* in my hair," said Lew, giving his shoulder an affectionate squeeze and setting the refilled mug down on the conference table. "Take your time, Doc, I like having you around."

No sooner had she settled back into her chair when the phone on her desk rang. "Yes, Marlaine," said Lew to the switchboard operator, stationed at the department's front desk. "Oh? Oh ... sure, send her in. And I'm expecting Ray Pradt to arrive sometime soon as well. Please send him right in when he gets here, okay? Thank you."

Rolling her eyes, she put the phone down and said, "*Doctor* Patience Schumacher is here and demanding to see me ASAP."

"Doctor, hmm," said Osborne, the title warring with his memories of a much younger Patience Schumacher. Well, Lew, you've been expecting this."

"Yeah, well, nice of her to call ahead."

"Time for me to skedaddle," said Osborne getting to his feet. "If the daughter is anything like her old man this won't be fun. That gentleman was one demanding sonofabitch. He'd be up from Chicago for the summer, have a toothache all day but not call the office until after I'd left and then torture my poor receptionist until she would give him my home number.

"Twice I opened the office after hours for him. And wouldn't you know—that jerk would take a *year* to pay. In fact," said Osborne tilting his chin up in thought, "there was one year he never did pay. And the man was worth *millions*. I got so tired of that razzbonya, I sicced him on poor Doc Metternich."

"Ha!" said Lew with a snort, "that is exactly why you are going to sit right back down, Deputy Osborne. I need someone who has some history here. And given how well you know Ray, it may be that between the two of us we can smooth some feathers and keep this issue from escalating."

"I have an idea," said Osborne. "We could offer a plea bargain of sorts. Make Ray guide them fishing for a day to make up for the drive-by scattering. They, in turn, have to listen to his jokes. Payback for their lack of basic human kindness."

Lew gave him the dim eye. "And one sure recipe for disaster."

Osborne shrugged. If the daughter was as arrogant as the father, Ray just may have the potential to drive her out of her mind. He grinned at the thought.

On hearing a loud knocking on the closed door of her office, Lew sighed and got to her feet.

Patience Schumacher was one of those unfortunate women who inherited her father's looks. If Osborne's estimate was even close, she stood a good six foot two. But where the old man had been a star basketball player in his youth—long, tall and lanky—Patience was long, tall and just plain big. Big-boned and big-breasted, with legs the diameter of an oak all wrapped in a charcoal grey business suit. The tailoring was good but optical fashion illusions can only go so far

Her hair, a tweedy mix of brown and grey, was cut so close to her skull that Osborne wondered if she trimmed it herself with an electric razor. Squirrel cheeks emphasized the massiveness of her Schumacher head and intense brown eyes darted around the room like a rodent searching for acorns.

Her cheeks were flushed with emotion and her voice was low, husky and loud as she pumped Lew's hand saying, "Good morning, Officer," then turned on her heel to stride across the room towards Osborne with a hand extended. She threw a black fur coat over the chair beside him and said, "Sheriff, *so good of you* to see us this morning." The husky voice came with a purr both ingratiating and seductive. Osborne wondered if she spoke to women that way.

Clearing his throat, he stood up from behind the conference table and placing both hands on the back of his chair, he said, "Sorry, I'm just a deputy and Chief Ferris there," he nodded towards Lew, "runs the Loon Lake Police Department."

"Oh." Patience swung back around to face Lew. "I just assumed ..." She had dropped the purr. "Of course, I should have known. But you look so familiar," she said looking back at Osborne. She paused a beat then said, "Oh, now I remember. You're Dr. Paul Osborne. You used to be our family's summer dentist years ago—right?"

"Yes, but I am retired from my practice and assist Chief Ferris when there are forensic matters such as dental records that require analysis."

"Dr. Osborne helps in other ways too when my department is shorthanded," said Lew, interrupting in a brisk tone as she beckoned for Patience to take one of the two chairs in front of her desk. "I'm Chief Lewellyn Ferris, and I am a police officer, not the county sheriff. Because it is located within the Loon Lake Township, your property is under our jurisdiction. So, please, have a seat."

"Excuse me? Am I in the right place?" asked an unfamiliar male voice. A man Osborne had never seen before stood waiting in the doorway.

"Charles, sweetheart, please, come in, come in," said Patience, turning towards him. The purr again. "My husband. We drove two cars," she said, looking back at Lew as if an explanation was needed for their separate arrivals. "Hurry, sweetie. Remember, I have to be at the college in half an hour." She pointed to the other chair in front of Lew's desk. "Here, hon, I saved you a place."

Osborne was struck by the woman's voice—quite the opposite of her father's, which could fill a room with booming commands.

While Patience's purr tempered her masculine appearance it didn't soften the visual impact. Was it her voice that had attracted her husband? Or the money? Osborne's daughters often kidded "an ugly rich man is not ugly." Does the same hold true for a homely rich woman?

Osborne struggled to reconcile his memories of Patience with the woman in front of him. As a teenager, she was so shy that on the few occasions her late mother brought her to his dental office, he had difficulty getting more than a mumble out of the kid. Perhaps because of the shyness, it came as no surprise that she entered the convent immediately after graduating from high school.

It was maybe ten years after that that Osborne learned from her father that Patience had left the convent, gone on to graduate school in business administration and was, at that time, working in the family's freight and warehousing business located in suburban Chicago. Osborne wondered if the officious tone and over-hearty mannerisms that she was exhibiting today might not be a mask for incredible shyness. Assuming she may have had to report to her father, that wouldn't surprise him. He could just hear the old man badgering his daughter to "take command, girl! Speak up!"

"And you are …?" asked Lew, leaning across her desk to shake hands with the man who was even taller than his wife. Later she would replay what occurred in the next few minutes: Was it his slim build or the athletic ease with which he crossed the room? The high cheekbones or the firm thrust to his chin? Maybe it was the soft grey eyes that met and held hers? Or the casual insouciance of the ponytail slung over one shoulder. 'Cool' is the word the registered as he approached.

Whatever the source of the visual chemistry, Lew felt herself drawn in to his gaze. She wasn't sure but he seemed to hold her hand just a touch too long. An unwelcome flush spread across her cheeks.

From the opposite side of the desk, Osborne watched the man as he reached to shake Lew's hand. Winter pale skin, watery, red-rimmed eyes and a stubble of beard emphasized gaunt features. A ponytail of lank grey hair hung over one shoulder and he walked with a slump as if trying to minimize his height. Osborne wondered if he was well. Either that or the guy didn't get outdoors much.

In contrast to his wife's executive appearance, the husband wore faded jeans that hung off his hip bones and a navy blue sweatshirt so old it was frayed at the cuffs and had long since lost its elasticity around the waist. Conspicuous down the front of the sweatshirt and the jeans were dark stains as if from grease. Random streaks and dabs of bright yellow, Irish green and orange intermingled with the grease spots. Over one arm, he carried a beige shearling coat that looked brand-new and expensive.

"Oh, I'm sorry," said Patience, interrupting before the man could answer Lew, "this is my husband, Charles." After a pause during which neither Lew nor Osborne said a word because they were so busy staring at the guy, she added, "Charles is an artist—he paints."

Ah, thought Osborne, recalling that he may have heard something along that line several months ago. Was it one of his McDonald's buddies who had mentioned that Patience Schumacher had "*finally* found a husband"? He'd have to check it out.

"Chief Lewellyn Ferris, Mr ...?" said Lew, introducing herself.

"Mason, Charles *Mason*," said the man, answering her implied question.

"I see. Please, both of you sit. Well, I have your complaint here," said Lew, hoping against hope that she was no longer blushing. She made sure to look down as she opened the folder on her

desk and clearing her throat, said, "I've asked Ray Pradt to join us this morning. He should be here any moment and I thought a full explanation of why he was on your property might help resolve—"

"That's not why we're here," said Patience, hitching her chair forward and leaning towards Lew. "I'm being stalked. Someone is entering our home when we're not there and I have reason to believe the same someone has been in my office at the college. I'm very worried." No more purr.

"Dr. Schumacher is convinced she is being stalked," said Charles, repeating his wife's words. "We need your help—"

"We want to apologize to Mr. Pradt," said Patience. "We overreacted when we saw him down by our boathouse. We thought he was my stalker."

"This certainly changes things," said Lew, closing the file and scrutinizing the faces of the two people in front of her. Before she could say more there was a knock at the office door.

"I'll get it," Osborne said, rising from his chair.

"That'll be Ray," said Lew.

Osborne moved to cross the room as the door flew open and Ray, looking quite civilized in black gabardine slacks, a brown leather belt with a bronze walleye for a buckle and a red and black checked Pendleton shirt, rushed in. He waved his right hand, which was clutching sheets of paper. Like a stiff wind out of the north he blew by Osborne—but not so fast that his neighbor couldn't see that something had changed. Something wasn't right ...

"Here you are ... all ... the facts," said Ray, slamming the papers down on Lew's desk without a glance at Patience Schumacher and her husband. "I Googled 'wildcat scatterings' and ...," he said, his voice rising as he spoke, "this printout *proves* that a wild-cat scattering ...," he paused to raise his right index finger and say, "is a ... *totally* legitimate way to dispose of human ashes.

Wildcat scatterings are very common and *no one* gets arrested. Even the FDA and the EPA say there's no health hazard—ashes are mineral based.

"Right here," he stabbed an accusing index finger at a spot on the first printed page, "it tells you *right here* that not only do forty percent of people today want to be cremated ... but last year at least one hundred and thirty five *thousand* families scattered ashes ... *wherever* they chose. Power back to the people for their loved ones.

"And *that* ... is what my visit to your property was all about." Only with his last words did Ray turn defiant eyes on Patience and her husband.

"For heaven's sake, people," he said, "all I scattered at your place was five pounds of an elderly widow whose family was trying to follow her wishes that she be able to join her beloved late husband. She and her children had already scattered his ashes over the lake where he loved to fish—"

"Mr. Pradt," said Patience, holding both palms up in surrender, "will you please calm down? We came to say that we're sorry about last night. We were just explaining to Chief Ferris that someone has been breaking into our house so when we saw you—we overreacted."

"Really?" said Ray, relaxing as he let a smile spread across his face.

Oh, no, thought Osborne, realizing what it was that had seemed off kilter: Ray was clean-shaven. He had shaved off his beard.

Chapter 11

"If that's settled," said Patience, getting to her feet, "I'm afraid I have to leave. I have a meeting in twenty minutes. Charles can answer any questions you might have."

"Excuse me, Dr. Schumacher—but you are *not* leaving," said Lew. "Please, sit down and we will continue this discussion." Before Patience could argue, Lew raised a hand and said, "Look, I understand you may have a busy day. We all do. But right now I need *both* you and your husband to answer questions. You do not rush in here, allege someone is stalking you, and then dash off to a meeting.

"Now …," said Lew, pausing as Patience remained seated on the edge of her chair as if still planning to leave, "you have made a serious allegation that could lead to a felony arrest. So I suggest you call your colleagues and have them cancel that meeting or at least move it back a couple hours. You *are* president of Wheedon Technical College, correct?"

"Yes, I am but—"

"Need a phone?"

"Good, I'm glad that's taken care of," said Lew. Patience had used her own cell phone to reach her secretary and have the meeting moved to late that afternoon. "Dr. Osborne, Ray—do you two mind sitting in on this?"

"Fine with me," said Osborne.

"Umm ... okay," said Ray, looking down at his cell phone to see if he had messages. "I might get called out though."

"This shouldn't take long," said Lew. Turning her attention back to Patience and Charles, she said, "Mr. Pradt and Dr. Osborne are deputies who help out when my department needs extra staff. They are long-time Loon Lake residents and know many people in the area. All *kinds* of people." A quick grin along with her emphasis on the word "kinds" made it clear that the good, the bad and the ugly were on their radar.

Turning in her chair to face Osborne and Ray, Patience said, "Thank you, gentlemen. I appreciate you're taking an interest in this."

"Now let's start at the beginning," said Lew, raising a pen over the long, narrow reporter's notebook she liked to use. "When did you *first* become aware that you were being stalked?"

Patience gave her husband a questioning look. "Oh ... about a month ago or so. Charles, would you agree?"

"That's about when you told me for the first time that you had the feeling someone was watching you," said Charles.

"Let's pinpoint this. When was that exactly?" asked Lew.

"Oh, maybe three weeks ago or so."

"But no specific day and time?"

"Not really."

Lew tilted her head to give Patience a puzzled look. "All right, Dr. Schumacher. Do you recall *where* you were when you became aware you were being stalked?"

"Well," said Patience, "that's the problem. I just *feel* someone is watching me *all the time*. When I come and go from my home, even when I'm *in* our house—but I never see him" Her husky voice faltered and, leaning forward as if her posture could convince Lew she was telling the truth, she said, "I can't see the man but I know he's there."

Osborne glanced down to see she was gripping the black leather folder in her lap so tightly her knuckles had turned white. Appearing uncomfortable with his wife's words, Charles shifted in his chair, his soft eyes seeking Lew's as if to convey a secret message.

Again a spark of something. The guy had charisma, Lew would admit that.

"Has there been any damage or theft at your home?" asked Lew, clearing her thoat. "Locks broken? Your security system tampered with?"

"We have no security system," said Patience. "That's why we moved here. We feel—or we *felt*, anyway—safe. Half the time we don't even lock our doors. Ever since I was a child, coming to Loon Lake in the summertime, this town has seemed to be a lovely community with lovely people. Why would we need a security system?"

Lew studied the top of her desk for a long moment before saying, "I suggest you lock your doors."

"We have—I mean, *I* have," said Charles. "Ever since Patience started worrying over this, I have made sure our doors are locked at night and whenever no one is home. But we don't have a security system."

"Let's go back to damage or theft," said Lew. "Anything unusual or missing from your home? Any tampering with your cars—evidence someone has been in or around the garage? The boathouse? Any person you are aware of who might be holding a grudge against you? Or your wife?"

"No," said Patience and Charles simultaneously.

Lew shook her head. "Then what makes you so sure you're being stalked?"

"I wish we could give you tangible proof and I know we sound nuts—but Charles and I agree—don't we, sweetheart?" Patience looked at her husband, who gave a reluctant nod. "We *sense* that someone is entering our home when neither of us is there. The only real evidence we have is that one time the laptop computer in my home office was left on."

"You agree, Charles?" asked Lew. "It wasn't left on by mistake by either of you?"

"No ... I really don't think so," said Charles. "Patience, I think you should tell them about your office at the college."

"Oh, well, I'm not sure about that." Patience threw a look of dismay at her husband.

"Tell them anyway." It was the first time Charles had sounded authoritative.

"Well ... okay. Chief Ferris, I am pretty sure someone goes into my office at the college when I'm traveling, away at meetings or in the evenings after hours. But," she shrugged, "thing is that could be a staff person who just needs a computer. We have an open door policy at the college and nothing has ever been missing."

"What about the college security?" said Lew. "You must have security personnel and cameras there?"

"No security cameras. We're a college, not a shopping mall," said Patience. "You have to realize my father endowed the college because he wanted a comfortable setting in a region that desperately needed a technical college where students can learn construction, plumbing, electronics, computer repair, CAD/CAM design, welding—all the basic building trades and skills that rural communities need. We have only three hundred and fifty students who all work hard and our faculty has impeccable credentials. These are not people who would steal or hurt one another."

"So you have an honor system," said Lew.

"Yes. I can't think of anyone at the college I don't trust. Even our maintenance crew has been with us since we opened the campus five years ago."

"All right. Let's go back to square one. You have no tangible evidence or sightings of a specific individual following you but you are convinced that you are being watched, correct?"

Patience nodded.

Lew continued, "Do you have a sense they mean to do harm?"

"If you're wondering am I fantasizing a guardian angel, no," said Patience. "I feel threatened. I don't even walk after dark anymore."

Lew set down the pen with which she had been taking notes and said in a kind voice, "Dr. Schumacher, I suggest you hire a private security firm to keep an eye out for anyone approaching your property. I'm afraid that until you have something more concrete, we can't help you.

"The Loon Lake Police Department—*and* the county sheriff's office—we are all severely understaffed for the next ten days with the international fishing tournament taking place. While we have reinforcements from the surrounding towns and counties, we just don't have the personnel—"

A sudden buzzing from the purse alongside Patience' chair prompted her to reach down for her cell phone and check the incoming call.

"Oh, dear, it's my lawyer," she said. "I really must return the call and arrange to speak with him later. Would you mind? I promise it won't take more than a few minutes."

"You'll need to step into the hall and use the conference room across the way if you want privacy," said Lew.

"Thank you," said Patience, getting to her feet.

The room seemed half empty after Patience left. No one spoke. Lew gathered up the papers Ray had dropped on her desk and set them to one side. Osborne cleared his throat. Ray checked his watch, then his cell phone.

"May I share something before my wife returns?" asked Charles, getting to his feet and walking across the room to close the door she had left open. He walked back to Lew's desk before saying in a low voice, "You should know that my wife is under tremendous stress right now. There are budget problems at the college, which are the result of a series of computer malfunctions that are costing a fortune. Patience feels wholly responsible even though it is certainly not her fault.

"The call from the lawyer? She's trying to convince the executor of her father's estate to release more funds to the college endowment in order to cover the costs of new equipment.

"While that situation is getting worse by the day, she is a nervous wreck when she is home, too." He hesitated then said, "I don't know if she is hallucinating or what but late last month she accused me of stealing from her. She was convinced that I had somehow accessed one of her bank accounts. There *was* an error, but it was a computer glitch at the bank." Charles paused, crossed his arms and stared down at his feet, thinking. He looked up. "To be perfectly frank, I'm not sure how much more *I* can take."

"Is she on meds of any kind?" asked Osborne.

"Patience takes quite a selection of vitamins every day but nothing more potent than that. At least as far as I know."

"Do you mind if I ask how long you've been married?" asked Lew.

"I don't mind·in the least," said Charles. "We met last year and were married … it'll be six months this next weekend," he gave a slight smile and raised his left hand as he spoke, displaying a wide gold wedding band. "She's been fine until all this pressure hit. It has really changed our lives. Used to be she would come home at night relaxed and happy. Now she's so rattled, it takes a glass or two of wine to calm her down."

The door to office opened and Patience walked over to her chair, "Sorry about that, everyone." She sat down saying, "You have my full attention, Chief Ferris. Charles, what did I miss?"

"I gave them a few more details concerning your office at the college," said Charles. "I also promised that we will keep the house secure and call 911 if we see or hear anything suspicious."

Osborne caught Lew's eye. Surprising how easily the guy lied to his wife. Sure he wanted to keep the level of upset down but still ...

"Regarding your office at the college, Dr. Schumacher," said Lew. "If you think someone is entering without permission—why not have a security camera installed? The cost will be well worth the peace of mind if you discover you have nothing to worry about."

Patience swung her head towards her husband as she said, "What did you say, Charles? Did you tell them this is all in my head? You did, didn't you!" She stood, both hands covering her face and half-sobbed in a muffled voice, "I give up. No one believes me." Her shoulders shook as she cried silent tears.

"Of course I do, Patty," said Charles as he got to his feet and reached to put a supportive arm around his wife. "All I said was that you are under a lot of stress at work and this isn't helping. That's all. Chief Ferris needs to know that." He stroked her back as he spoke.

Patience wavered, then reached for her purse and a Kleenex, which she used to dab at her face. She blew her nose. "You're right, Charles, I am so sorry. You are so good to me."

"Chief Ferris," said Charles, continuing to stroke his wife's arm. "Do you need anything more from us right now?"

"This is a start," said Lew. "Enough for today."

Patience sniffled and got to her feet. "Thank you for your time," said Charles, holding his wife's fur for her to slip into.

"Dr. Schumacher, Mr. Mason," said Lew as she walked them to the door, "Here are two of my cards with my cell phone number. One for each of you. The cell phone is on 24/7. I trust you won't use it unless you have a sighting of the person— or people—behind your concern. Call 911 first, then my cell. I would like that alert ASAP. Does that help?"

"You think there could be more than one person behind this?" said Patience, tucking her wet Kleenex into her coat pocket.

"I have no idea," said Lew, "but I have learned to trust intuition. So we will work with you until we figure this out."

Patience was so relieved her eyes shimmered with tears. "Thank you," she said. "Thank you."

"Yes," said Charles, pausing to shake the hands of Lew, Osborne and Ray as his wife hurried on down the hall. "Thank you for listening."

"Mr. Mason," said Osborne, "before you leave, may I have a look at that wedding ring of yours? I've worked in gold and silver extensively in my dental practice and that is quite the ring."

"Thank you," said Charles, holding his left hand out for everyone to see, "I designed both our rings. No stones, just wide bands beaten with a special mallet that I like to use. It's 18kt gold. The best you can get these days."

"Very handsome," said Osborne. "I haven't seen anything like it."

"Take a look at Patience's ring next time. It's wider and you can see the pattern better. I am quite proud of it."

"So, Lewellyn, what do you think?" asked Osborne when she had closed the door.

"I think we listen and wait. It would appear that Dr. Schumacher is neurotic if not clinically paranoid—and that may be. If that is what it is, then all we have is an emotionally troubled person who needs professional help. But if that is not the case and she *is* being stalked and we do not listen, then we have a victim.

"We could have a homicide—or, if someone is out to drive her crazy—a suicide. Patience strikes me as pretty darn fragile."

"In other words, why risk the worst?" asked Osborne.

"Exactly. Though I sure as hell wish her timing was better," said Lew. "Hey," she said, turning her attention to the man still seated at the conference table, "Ray, what's your impression?"

"Huh?" Startled, Ray looked up from his cell phone, which he was checking for the umpteenth time. "She's very tall."

"Thank you. That's a *big* help," said Lew. Her eyes narrowed as she said, "I would like to know more about those two. They seem rather an odd couple to me."

"I'll ask around," said Osborne. "I know I heard something not too long ago."

"Thanks, Doc. Meantime, you two, I have Roger and Todd interviewing the property owners with land within a three-mile radius of the Merriman Trails. I figure Kathy Beltner could not have gone much farther than that even if she decided to snowshoe off trail.

"Ray, you will get out there *now* while the sun is out, won't you? Those trails have been closed to accommodate us and I've already had two calls from the DNR. They have some upset skiers ..."

"Yep, I'm on my way. Got a trail map in the truck and I'll cover as much territory as I can before the sun goes down. Doc, you coming?"

"On the condition you tell me why you keep checking that damn cell phone."

"The producers of ICE MEN said they'll call everyone who makes the first cut today. I'm hoping to hear."

An hour later, Lew's cell phone pinged with a text message: "Got a minute? Charles." She hit the "call" button and Charles Mason answered.

"Is this an emergency?" asked Lew.

"Hi," said Charles in a tone Lew found seductive and alarming, "I thought we might talk some more about, oh, Patience and—"

"If it's not an emergency, Mr. Mason," said Lew, enunciating each word, "I don't have time." And clicked her phone off.

Lew pondered the call and her visceral response to the man. Once before in her life she had found herself attracted to a man like Charles—physically appealing and with a certain intensity in his eyes and manner. She almost married the guy, but a minor disagreement blew up between them, exposing the fact he was borderline schizophrenic. It was a hard lesson learned but she remembered it now.

Could she be dealing with two disturbed units in one household? Time for background checks on Patience and Charles, especially Charles.

CHAPTER 12

Osborne bent to strap on his snowshoes. He had had them for years and never failed to admire the workmanship in the handmade wooden frames with their varnished rawhide webbing. Some people—like Erin, who had outfitted all his grandchildren in aluminum snowshoes—pooh-poohed vintage models. They preferred modern versions: machine-generated with aluminum, plastic and vinyl fittings.

But Osborne held fast to his antiques and enjoyed badgering his daughter with, "Erin, snowshoes like mine are true to the culture of the Ojibway nation whose blood runs in your father's Metis veins. If you valued the traditions of our ancestors, you would wear snowshoes like mine."

"Yeah, right, Dad." And on she would walk in lighter, shorter, narrower snowshoes: her loss.

Hunched over as he sat on the tailgate of his truck, parked next to Osborne at the trailhead, Ray had his gloves off as his fingers worked fast to strap snowshoes on over his Sorel boots. He had arrived late and Osborne suspected he had stopped by his trailer to check email in hopes he had received news on-line from the ICE MEN producers. From the expression on his face he hadn't heard anything and Osborne knew better than to ask.

"I can't believe you bought those," said Osborne, staring down at his neighbor's feet. He was dumbfounded that even Ray had bought into the aluminum snowshoe craze.

Giving Osborne's snowshoes a dubious look, Ray shrugged and said, "Sure you want to wear those old things, Doc? With that mist frozen over last night's snowfall—we'll be on hard stuff out there."

"I'll be fine," said Osborne. Determined to prove the point, he marched bow-legged across the parking lot to the snowshoe trail. He started down the trail only to discover Ray was right: the surface was slick as an ice rink. At the first dip in the trail, his snowshoes slid out from under him. Grabbing the branches of a nearby alder bush, he managed to stumble sideways without falling.

"C'mon, Doc," said Ray speeding up from behind, "you walk like an injured loon in those contraptions. You're gonna hurt yourself."

"Too late to do anything about it now," said Osborne, dusting the snow off his pants. He was not looking forward to the next few hours if this was how it would be. With a grunt, he yanked on the leather strap holding the heel of his left boot and started forward again only to slip and fall to one side.

"Damn, that snow is hard," he said as he sat on the trail trying to figure out how to get back to a standing position without killing himself.

"Doc, stop," said Ray, "take those damn things off and let's walk back to the truck. I have an extra pair you can use. They'll grip this crust so you won't slide and break a leg. C'mon, back to the truck, old man. Won't take more'n five minutes."

Moments later, strapped into the smaller snowshoes, Osborne skimmed over the snow. He hated to admit it, but Ray was right. Even on the treacherous downhill slopes, the snowshoes caught and held without skidding. He had no trouble keeping up. But he was betraying his ancestors. Hmm, would Erin be kind when she heard he'd capitulated? Likely not. But eating crow beats recovering from broken bones.

Pausing at a fork, Ray studied the trail in both directions before saying, "Oh, brother. This is not good. Chief Ferris wants us to find some sign of the route Kathy Beltner took last night but I gotta tell ya this hard glaze is no help. It hides damn near everything."

He bent to push a mitt through the crisp upper layer, which cracked to expose granular snow just under the surface. "Ouch," he said, "try walking through this without snowshoes and it'll take the skin right off your shins."

After brushing away about five inches of loose snow, Ray's mitt hit another hardened layer. The alternating snow and mist of the previous twenty-four hours was going to make tracking difficult if not impossible—and they both knew it.

"We have to at least try," said Osborne. "For the family's sake."

"I know. Tell you what," said Ray, pulling out a trail map and holding it so Osborne could see, "if you'll go that direction, I'll take this and let's meet up at the warming hut down here where the south loop crosses the west loop ski trails. She had to have gone one of these two ways, right?"

"As far as I can see from the map, this is the only trail open to snowshoeing—all the others are marked for skating or diagonal skiing. You know how upset skiers get if anyone snowshoes on their groomed trails."

"But she wouldn't be the first person to wander off trail in heavy snow like we had."

"Doc, that has to be what happened. It's the only answer. My thought is that if we see any sign of someone, whether it was Kathy Beltner or anyone else, going off trail—that's where we go.

So try to see as far off trail as possible—check for broken branches, depressions in the snow cover—you know the drill. But if you see something, mark the spot and come get me. We go together just in case ..."

Osborne set off down his assigned trail. He hadn't gone ten minutes before he paused to inhale the pristine air and berate himself for not snowshoeing more often: the exquisite silence of the forest, the remarkable serenity, the absolute freedom. On snowshoes, you can go wherever you please—over lakes and streams, deep into woods; you can bushwhack through alders, birch and evergreens; you can walk through swamps impassable in warmer seasons and where there are breathtaking vistas from points impossible to reach in the summertime.

He had forgotten, too, how winter changes forests. As if rebelling against the grey slab of a winter sky, the red pines seem more stately, the balsam spires more pointed, the towering hemlocks more threatening.

Osborne walked on, studying the snow-covered fields along the trail. The only sound might be the soft whoosh of his snowshoes but he was not alone. The tiny footprints of voles sped this way and that before diving back under the snow. Chewed off tips of pine boughs and small pinecones littering the trail betrayed the presence of red squirrels and porcupines. He and Ray might be the only humans on the trail system, but the forest was as busy as a Costco warehouse.

A deposit of scat packed with deer hair caused him to slow and scan the snow for the paw prints of a timber wolf. No luck: the hard surface gave up no trace of the predator's path. But he did spot a well-traveled deer trail running parallel to the snowshoe trail for a short distance before veering off towards the vast cedar swamp that anchored the north end of a small lake, which meant he was closing in on the warming hut.

By the time he met up with Ray the icy light of the waning sun warned they were running short of time. The warming hut was a simple structure—three walls of hand-hewn logs with benches attached and a tarpaper roof overhead: shelter for winter athletes before tackling their next five miles. One end was open to the outdoors and a small rock pedestal held a fire pit. Ray had a modest fire going and was resting on a bench while checking his cell phone.

"Any news?"

"No." The dejection in his voice worried Osborne.

"So what if you don't get it—that was a long shot and you know it. Plus that reality show is probably a low rent operation. Save your talents for the networks."

Ray gave him a rueful smile. Osborne shook his head. For reasons he never understood, Ray had long ago decided that given half a chance he could be a real star on cable TV. When Osborne needed entertainment all he had to do was drop by Ray's trailer and listen to his neighbor badmouth the guys on the OUTDOORS NETWORK.

"I don't know, Doc. "ICE MEN is the best shot I've had in years. How often do you see ESPN in the Northwoods? Those guys are all about bass tournaments in goddamn Alabama, y'know?"

"By the way," asked Osborne, "is that why you shaved off your beard?"

"Uh-huh. I thought it would help if I looked my absolute best. Dressed nicely, well-shaven. My mom hated my beard. She always said I'd be much better looking without it. But I made a mistake. I heard one of the casting producers say they were disappointed I didn't show up looking like I did when they had sign-ups at the library the other day."

"Ah, they want the old 'jack pine savage' type?"

"C'mon, I don't look *that* bad, Doc."

"Not to me and the rest of us in Loon Lake but to city folk, maybe."

"Yeah, so now I look like an average Joe, is that it?"

Osborne shrugged. What could he say? A handsome average Joe, but not the standout Ray Pradt with the cascade of auburn and gray curls in his beard that matched the untamed mop on his head. The hair, the beard, the laughing eyes: that was the Ray Pradt who rarely failed to catch the eye of an attractive woman. And if television people know anything, they know what women want.

Osborne was chagrined for his friend. Shaving the beard probably was a bad decision and one that couldn't be reversed.

After a few more minutes warming in front of the toasty fire, they were ready to return to the parking lot. This time Ray wanted them to switch trails, with Osborne taking the route out that Ray had come in on. Ray would take the trail Osborne had just followed. "You never know what you might see going the other direction," said Ray, "and it never hurts to try new eyes."

"What about the swamp?" asked Osborne. "You'll see a deer trail running in that direction. Should we come back tomorrow and check that out?"

"Heavens no. I can't imagine Kathy Beltner would have snowshoed into the swamp," said Ray. "Unless they want to wade home most of the year, I don't know of anyone living back that way either. That swamp is all wetland with some deep holes.

"No, my hunch is we're looking for the nut who parked on the access road and was hiding on the trail just waiting for a woman to rob or ... you know. Like that guy who attacked the runner out on Crescent Lake Road a few years back."

As he spoke, Ray pulled two headlamps from the pack he was wearing around his waist. "Here, Doc, wear this and you won't have a problem once the sun sets."

"Thanks, are these new?"

"Yep, got 'em for myself for Christmas. They work real well, too. You'll be surprised." After adjusting the straps of the headlamp so it fit tight over the earflaps on his knit hat, Osborne reached up to switch it on. "Give it one more twist, Doc," said Ray, "it has a green light, too, one that catches the definition in the snow better."

"Got it," said Osborne and started on his way. He wasn't a big fan of being in the woods after dark in the winter: Too many opportunities to hit an icy patch or be tackled by a great horned owl on the hunt.

But to his relief, as the sky darkened the beam from the headlamp lit an area quite wide in diameter. The green light defined the drifts and hollows in the snow so well that he could see the tiny footprints of forest critters with ease. If there was any sign of anyone veering off the trail, the light would catch it.

Osborne paused to savor the peace of the darkening forest. Within seconds, he was struck by an unusual feature of the headlamp: the green light reflected off eyes watching him— reflected without frightening their owners. So many eyes he decided not to linger.

Trudging along, he was aware of being observed by multiple pairs that were knee high or lower: rabbits, squirrels, mice. Coming around a stand of balsam he met two pair shoulder height, also not spooked. These had to be deer convinced they were safely hidden behind the screen of evergreen branches.

He was halfway to the parking lot when he spotted a newcomer, one whose eyes were just *below* shoulder height. These eyes stayed with him all the way to the trail's end. Even after reminding himself that wolves only attack the weak, he hoped the predator was more interested in venison than retired dentists.

While stepping out of his snowshoes, it crossed his mind that Patience Schumacher might not be hallucinating: *you never know when you might be watched.*

Ray was sitting in the front seat of his pick-up. He held his cell phone in one hand and stared at it.

"No call?" asked Osborne, hating to ask the question.

"Nope. Oh, and I didn't see any sign on my way back either. Feel like a Cub Scout trying to track in these conditions. What about you?"

"No luck but I sure saw plenty of critters watching me. You didn't mention that the green light wouldn't scare them off."

"Sweet, isn't it? At least you got something good out of the afternoon." The despair in his voice was unmistakable.

"Now, Ray, don't beat yourself up—"

"See you later, Doc," said Ray before Osborne could finish. "You'll call the Chief? She'll be disappointed." He had turned the ignition and was backing up before Osborne could return the borrowed snowshoes.

Watching as his friend turned the truck around and drove out of the parking lot without a wave, Osborne's concern grew. It isn't just wolves lurking out there. Other demons stalk—and Ray had his share.

Once he was back on the county highway, Osborne reached for his cell phone to punch in Lew's number. "Plus our friend is in bad shape," he said after reporting the frustrating results of the afternoon. "It appears he did not get hired for the reality show. Lew, I don't remember seeing him so depressed."

"Must be something in the air today, Doc. My daughter just called. Looks like she and her husband have split. Suzanne is in her car headed this way and she does not sound good. By the way, was I ...," she paused. "Did I somehow behave unprofessionally during our meeting with Patience and her husband, Charles?"

"I'm not sure what you mean, Lew. I thought you handled the meeting well. Why?"

"I had a call from Charles later. He texted me, too. Just wanted to chat."

"He wanted 'to chat?'" said Osborne, sounding dumbfounded. "Where did that come from? You specifically told both of them to use your cell phone only if they saw—"

"Right. Only if they saw the person—or persons—stalking Patience. That's what I thought I said. This is too weird, Doc— I think the guy was hitting on me."

CHAPTER 13

Osborne was in the middle of a dream when he heard a robin singing only to realize it was Lew's cell phone ringing. She scrambled out of the bed to grab for the phone. From where he lay half asleep Osborne could hear the woman scream on the other end of the line.

"Ohmygod, he's in our house! Somewhere in the house! He's here, he's here!" It was Patience Schumacher.

"Have you called 911?" asked Lew, wrapping a bathrobe around her with one hand while holding tight to the cell phone. Hitting speakerphone so Osborne could hear too, she jerked a thumb towards the kitchen—a signal he needed to call the switchboard on the landline. Covering the mouthpiece, she said, "Doc, I want confirmation we got a patrol car on the way ..."

"Patience, give me the phone." It was Charles, his raspy voice loud enough that Osborne could hear as he ran from the bedroom to the kitchen. "Hello, Chief Ferris? Yes, we called 911, Patience has my cell phone and is staying on the line with the operator but now we're locked in the bedroom. I don't know what to do—"

Osborne reached for the landline hanging near the kitchen door and heard Lew ask, "Where is the intruder?" He reached the night operator, who assured him that Roger should be arriving at the Schumacher's any moment. Osborne dashed back to the bedroom.

"... So you haven't seen anyone but you hear noises in the den?" asked Lew.

"Yes, a beeping noise every few minutes and the sound of drawers opening and closing. Right now ... it's quiet. They must be hiding here somewhere. Oh, I see headlights outside. Maybe that's the police? What should I do?"

"Stay right where you are and stay off your phone. I want you to keep this line free. I'll speak with the officer on our police radio—make sure that's who drove up—and call you right back."

"Roger?" said Lew seconds later into the police radio, "you're at the Schumacher's right? See a car there or parked anywhere nearby?

"No car," said Roger. "Driveway is empty. Garage closed."

"Any movement? Lights anywhere?" Lew was a master at dressing with one hand, though Osborne did help with her boots. While Lew talked, he threw on his own clothes.

"Nothing moving that I can see but haven't shone the floods yet," said Roger. "I see a light on behind curtains on the west end of the house. Otherwise house is dark."

"All right. Keep a close eye out. I should be there within ten minutes. I'm going to check on that light."

She punched in the number for the Schumacher's cell phone and Charles answered. "There is a light at the west end of your house—is that your den or the bedroom?"

"That's us in the bedroom. Den is at the back of the house behind the kitchen."

"Okay, Roger? The light you see is from their bedroom where they've locked themselves in. Do your best to see what you can with the floods but keep yourself out of harm's way."

"Will do."

Lew and Osborne made it to the Schumacher's in less than eight minutes. As they pulled up, Roger stepped out of the squad car and walked back to Lew's cruiser. "I haven't seen a thing. No movement, nothing. I scoured the front of the place with the floods but no luck so I turned them off. I can see better in the dark."

"Did you keep an eye on that boathouse?" said Lew, looking over Roger's shoulder as she got out of the car.

"Yep, didn't see nothin."

"Okay." Lew reached into the trunk for a large torchlight, which she switched on as she started towards the Schumacher's driveway. "Doc, you wait here with Roger. Call the Schumachers on your cell and tell them to stay on the line. I will approach the house along one side of the driveway—right where you see those shadows. If they hear someone moving inside, see if they can tell where that person might be."

"Careful, Lewellyn," said Osborne, "be very careful."

"Don't worry."

Torch off, she slipped into the darkness near the Schmacher's garage. The black parka made it easy for her to disappear into the shadows. Osborne, watching over the hood of Roger's squad car and with Charles on the line, held his breath. He noticed that Lew's boots left footprints in the light snow that had fallen during the night. His eyes searched the front yard but he could see no sign of other footprints. Odd. Had the intruder entered through the back of the house?

The midnight air was ice-cold and a mournful wind moved through the tops of the pines surrounding the two-story frame house. It had a wide veranda running across the front, which Lew had just begun to move across. Stooping low, she stopped to shine the torch through the first of four wide picture windows. When she was satisfied she could see nothing through that one, she moved on to the next.

"Do you hear anything?" Osborne asked Charles, keeping his voice low and his mouth close to the phone.

"Someone on the front porch."

"That's Chief Ferris—any movement *inside* the house?"

"Not right now, not that I can tell ..."

After looking long and hard through the fourth and final window, Lew turned off the torch and stood still, listening. She stepped off the end of the veranda into knee-deep snow that crunched as she moved. Osborne thought he heard a soft curse. Ray had been right—the surface was frozen hard enough to hurt.

At the back of the house, she paused to run the beam of the torch across the backyard. Signaling that she saw nothing, she returned to the veranda, crossed to the other side of the house and checked the backyard from that angle along with the garage and the east side of the house. She tried a side door—it was locked. She tried a door on the side of the garage and it was locked, too.

Back on the veranda, she knocked snow off her boots and walked to the front door where she knocked loudly, "Mr. Schumacher? This is Chief Ferris—please open the door."

A long pause before lights came on in the living room. Charles Schumacher appeared at the front door. He was wearing a dark-colored bathrobe over blue pajamas. At the sight of Lew, he opened the door wide and beckoned her inside. She turned and waved to Osborne, "Doc, Roger, come on in."

"No footprints around the house and the only tracks right now are mine in the driveway," said Lew. "Roger said it has been snowing since ten so anyone entering would have left some trace. I also tried the locks on all your doors—nothing open."

The Schumachers were sitting side by side on a living room sofa facing Lew. Both in their bathrobes, Patience was still shaking. "Someone was on my computer, I swear," she said, voice cracking as she pushed a wet Kleenex against her eyes.

"Show me," said Lew.

"All right," said Patience with a loud sniff. With that, everyone stood to follow her down a wide carpeted hallway to a woodsy den that held several upholstered chairs and a large desk on which sat a laptop computer connected to a wide-screen monitor. Behind the desk, against the wall, was a router and modem with all their lights flashing.

"Do you always leave your computer on overnight?" asked Lew.

"I like to turn it off," said Patience. "The techs at the college tell me to leave it on but I hate to waste electricity. The router and the modem stay on but not the laptop. I realize that doesn't make sense. When it comes to computers, I am technologically challenged." She gave a weak grin and Osborne realized how frightened she was. "I depend on our techs for everything."

"Tell me this—have you had any computer issues recently?"

"Kind of," said Patience, shooting a questioning look at Charles as if she wanted his approval to discuss something. "Um, someone has been emailing our students using my name and email and trying to sell them stuff—teeth whitener, smartphones, expensive textbooks. I can assure you that is not me doing that."

Charles' face seemed to fall as he said to Lew, "That is one of the issues that has been weighing on my wife. Someone is hacking into her email but no one, not even the woman who runs the computer tech department, can figure it out—much less stop it."

"I see," said Lew. She glanced down at her watch. "It's very late, folks. We all need some sleep. Now what we know is that no one has entered your home this evening—I guarantee that from checking outside and in. Do you think you can relax and get some sleep?"

"If we keep the bedroom door locked and chair up against it," said Patience in a grim tone.

"If it makes you feel better, do that. We'll talk late in the morning. I'd like to discuss this with our tech and see if he has time to check your computer set-up."

As if it had heard itself discussed, the laptop computer wheezed, darkened and shut down only to make a pinging noise as it booted back up. The speakers beeped and the CD-Rom drive opened and shut and opened and shut. Everyone watched, speechless.

CHAPTER 14

Bleary-eyed and desperately in need of a full night's sleep, Osborne shouldered his way through the door into McDonald's. It was six-thirty and the coffee crowd was already deep into their second and third cups of coffee.

"Hey, Doc," said a chorus of voices. "How's it going?"

Osborne waved off the question, got his first mug of coffee and plopped himself into a chair. "I am ... dead ... tired," he said, borrowing a speech pattern from Ray. "Beat. Too old for this."

That led to a series of raised eyebrows and half smirks. His buddies might know better than to crack tasteless jokes but the thought was in their eyes. And some of it was jealousy.

Osborne had to cackle. "Nah, not what you think, fellas. Lew got an emergency call just before midnight and we didn't get back until after three. By that time my adrenaline level made it impossible to get back to sleep."

Still those teasing eyes, so he changed the subject. "Say, who was it was saying about Patience Schumacher recently? Something about that guy she married?"

"That would be me," said Wayne French through a mouthful of sausage egg McMuffin. He wiped at his lips with a crumpled napkin before saying more. Osborne waited, but Wayne took another bite.

Wayne French was a general contractor who would work only in Loon Lake and even then only jobs outside the town proper. He refused jobs in Rhinelander or Eagle River because of what he considered "ridiculous building codes"—or was it "ridiculous building inspectors?" Osborne was too tired to remember.

"So ... I don't remember what I said exactly," said Wayne once the sandwich was gone, mopping crumbs off the table with his napkin. "All I know is she married this fellow that I hired to paint the interior walls of her house."

"You sure that's right?" asked Osborne. "I was told the man is an artist. He paints pictures. You know, like outdoor scenes or something."

"Oh ho," snorted Wayne, "maybe he does now. But when my crew did the work in that house of hers—had to tear out the wainscoting on the master bedroom ceiling twice before that woman was happy—hundred thousand dollars of time and materials and I ain't makin' that up! I hired Chuck to paint the walls and stain the moldings. That's how they met. Before the remodeling was done, they were engaged."

Osborne stared at him. "You're kidding. How long ago was this?"

"Less than a year ago. Why?"

"Just wondering," said Osborne. "Ran into the guy the other day and found him interesting."

"Interesting and bone broke," said Wayne. "Man, that sucker lucked out. Wish I could meet a woman with a million times my bank account. Hell, I'd think twice even if she did look like Patience Schumacher."

"C'mon, Wayne," said Osborne, shaking his head. "That's not kind. I'm sure those two have more in common than that."

"I dunno," said Wayne, going for a refill. "I been around enough I seen some weird pairings in my life and that one takes the cake."

"Where's he from? Around here somewhere?"

"Says he grew up on a dairy farm outside Rhinelander. Lived on the West Coast with his first wife, he said—but never would say what he did in those days. I just assumed he's made his way doing odd jobs. Gave me a P.O. box for his checks and never did give me a Social Security number. Said he'd take care of it."

"We're talking about the same guy, right?" asked Osborne. "Charles Mason."

"*Charles?* Hell, no. Chuck's how I know him."

The door to Lew's office was closed when Osborne arrived at seven thirty. He gave a light knock before opening and poked his head around the door to be sure it was okay to enter. She was on the phone and waved him in.

"Okay, thank you, tomorrow then. I'll inform the family," she said as she hung up. She looked up at Osborne saying, "The hearse will return Kathy Beltner's body to the funeral home tomorrow morning," she said. "They've finished the autopsy and just have the paperwork to complete."

"That's a relief," said Osborne. "I know Rob and his girls will appreciate the hearse, Lewellyn." She gave him a sidelong glance intended to dismiss the comment. Osborne was one of few people who knew that when autopsies were required to be conducted at a distance from Loon Lake, she paid for the hearse transport out of her own pocket. The town had no budget for that service and soon after her promotion to Chief, Lew discovered that Pecore shuttled victims who had died of unnatural causes in the back of his pickup truck.

"I refuse to allow abuse like that on my watch," Lew had said, and that was that.

"Surprise, surprise, Doc," said Lew, leaning on her elbows, fingers steepled. "No help from Wausau on this situation with Patience Schumacher and the computer issues. According to my best buddy down there," she said in a tone heavy with sarcasm, "if Internet fraud is involved, then it's for the Feds to work."

After mimicking the dismissive tone of the head of the Wausau Crime Lab, she fixed Osborne with a long look. The director of the crime lab made no secret of the fact that he believed women in law enforcement belonged behind a desk. No guns, no cruisers, no surveillance training "for girls." Hence no love was lost between Chief Lewellyn Ferris and the professional she had to rely on when the crime lab and its technicians were needed.

"Good. Gets that jerk off your back, Lew. I'd call the FBI right now," said Osborne.

"I did and that went nowhere. They think it's just a couple of college kids hacking in and they don't have time to bother with it. Plus they loaned their computer tech to Ironwood where some bank has had a rash of identity theft."

"But Ironwood is in Michigan!"

"That's what I said. All I could get out of the FBI agent this morning was that if we can find the student behind this, *then* they will step in. So we do the work, they handle the arrest and get the credit. Any way you look at it, I'm screwed."

"Maybe not you, but Patience Schumacher sure is. And her campus."

"Exactly." Lew's eyes widened. "Campus? *Campus.* There's a thought, Doc. Gina Palmer! Why didn't I think of her before? She was awarded a fellowship to teach computer-assisted investigative reporting this year at the School Of Journalism in Madison. I'll bet she's got a grad student who can help us out."

"Worth a try," said Osborne.

CHAPTER 15

"**H**ey, bad girl!" A husky voice with a mobster edge crackled over the speakerphone on Lew's desk. For Osborne, the staccato burst of harsh sound triggered an instant image—a pixie of a woman always in black. A cap of glossy straight black hair, glittering ebony eyes, a wicked sense of humor and that dark voice: Gina Palmer.

She didn't strike Osborne as an academic—someone adept at the sketchy politics of university life—though he knew she had talents unique in the world of journalism. Gina was one of few journalists mathematically inclined to design the software needed to support database-driven investigative reporting. From workman's comp to illegal processing of human tissue, she could tackle innocuous-appearing data and distill patterns both informative and damning.

"Yeah, well, I made one big mistake two months ago," Gina's voice came through the speakerphone, her signature staccato that made you feel like you were running to catch up instead of listening. "My appointment ran out end of December and for some crazy reason I accepted an offer to teach for another two years. I have a terrific team of grad students and our department just won a big grant from the federal government to continue developing investigative software for the FBI, CIA and NSA. Fun stuff. What are you folks up to?"

Lew waited before answering, not sure if Gina really was ready to listen—but it was a legitimate opening

"Hey," said Lew. "If I can squeeze a few bucks out of the budget, I sure could use help from you or your students on a case I have. The FBI should have taken it—computer fraud—but they've blown me off saying it's small potatoes and they're too busy. The situation is that we have a new tech college at the mercy of a hacker or team of hackers rampaging through their system."

"Tell me more," said Gina.

"Thank you," said Lew with a sigh of relief. "I would very much appreciate your feedback." She described the disturbances Patience Schumacher was experiencing with the computers in her home and at the college. "Sound like anything your team might help us with?"

"Help you? Tell you what," said Gina, sounding excited, "I've been looking for a case study like this to complete my dissertation. "Let me talk to my students—we're meeting later today—and see what I can round up. Meantime, why don't you see the computer tech on site at the college, someone we can coordinate with."

"Can you let me know the approximate cost when we talk next?" asked Lew.

"Maybe nothing," said Gina. "This could be considered research under the grants we just got. But I'll see. Hey, I got a small favor to ask. I got the utility bill for my cabin and it is way up. Could you ask Ray to check and see if the furnace is going crazy—or maybe the pump for my well has run amok? Something is out of whack—it's two hundred bucks over last month's."

"I'll ask Ray to check it out," said Osborne, leaning into the speakerphone.

"Thanks, Doc. Talk to you folks later."

Setting the phone down, Lewellyn Ferris beamed up at Osborne as she said, "Case study for a dissertation? I want to see a case study that shows the goddamn Wausau boys *and* the Feds a thing or two. This may be the last time they blow me off."

"As far as paying for Gina and her team," said Osborne. "I'll bet Patience Schumacher would be more than happy to subsidize their work."

Lew's eyes widened with happy speculation, "Doc, you are so right. I'll touch base with Patience this morning before I try squeezing another penny here. If she'll come through, the mayor will love me."

Ray's voice on Osborne's cell phone sounded far away if not slightly slurred. "Ray, you there and okay?"

"Yeah, what?"

"I'm in Lew's office and we just got off the phone with Gina Palmer. The last utility bill on her cabin was very high. She was hoping you could check her place out and see if something has been left on—the furnace, the water pump, something is not working right out there. Think you have time to check on that later today?"

The sound of bed covers rustling. "Doc, did you say Gina Palmer?"

"Right. Lew's got her helping out with a computer glitch out at the tech college—we'll be talking to her later. The sooner the better if you can manage it. Ray."

"Lemme get over to her cottage and shee what I can do." Again the worrisome slur.

"Thanks, hold on a second." Osborne covered the phone with his hand as he whispered to Lew, "Think of something. I'm worried he's drinking again. I could be wrong but—"

"Dinner. Invite him to my place for dinner tonight. Suzanne arrives this afternoon. No kids. She's feeling pretty low. Might help both of them to know they aren't the only one suffering. Sometimes sharing someone's else's pain helps you gain some perspective on your own life—know what I mean, Doc?

"And you know how Ray loves helping people out—let's put Suzanne on his radar and see if that might change his focus a little." Lew grinned. "It'll certainly change hers. Those two were just a few years apart in high school and I remember at least one of Suzanne's girlfriends had a crush on Ray. At the very least we'll have good food and a chance for pleasant conversation that may get both their minds off their respective problems for a short time."

"Good idea," said Osborne, taking his hand off the phone. "Ray, Chief Ferris would like for you to come to dinner at her farm this evening. Her daughter, Suzanne, is driving up from Milwaukee and she thought it would be nice to have a few friends over. Are you free?"

"Sure." Ray sounded surprised. "Want me to bring some walleyes?"

"Want him to bring walleyes?" said Osborne to Lew.

"No, just his gorgeous self."

Osborne repeated the instructions only to hear Ray say, "Then I'm bringing dessert. I have an apple pie in the freezer."

Clicking his phone off, Osborne said, "That helped. He started to sound a little better."

"Secret to a happy life is planning ahead," said Lew. "Now get out of here. I have things to do and places to go, Doc."

CHAPTER 16

O sborne was midway through the loaf of garlic bread that he was under orders to slice and butter when the kitchen door banged open. Knocking the snow off her boots with two swift kicks as she stayed huddled in her down coat, Suzanne Ferris-Meyer barged into the room. She slammed the door shut behind her and collapsed back against it.

"O-o-o-h, Mom, it is so freezing out there," she said pulling off her gloves. "I must be nuts to drive all this way when it's so damn cold. I'm such a wreck." Her shoulders slumped as she spoke. "My boss said to take a couple days off and—oh, hi," she said suddenly spotting Osborne, who was standing near the stove and half-hidden by a pot rack hanging in the middle of the room.

She acknowledged his presence with a hint of embarrassment. She might be a grown woman but she was sounding like a little kid who needed her mother. Osborne wondered if he shouldn't leave the room.

"Well, I am very happy you made it, and right on time for dinner," said Lew in a cheery voice. "Coat goes on a hook right behind you on the porch. Leave your boots there, too." She gave Osborne a glance that instructed him *not* to leave the room.

Waving her daughter towards the back porch, Lew continued tearing the lettuce for the salad, then leaned sideways to check on a large pot of water, which was close to boiling and sending tendrils of steam into the warm, well-lit kitchen.

"Sweetie, things are almost ready. We're waiting for one more guest for dinner," said Lew, dropping the last leaves of lettuce into a bowl and wiping her hands on her apron. "Come here, you," she said, opening her arms to embrace the young woman.

Osborne had met Suzanne only once before. Slimmer than her mother, Suzanne was about the same height with the same coloring. But where her mother had an unruly cap of dark curls, Suzanne wore her hair long, straight and pulled into a ponytail. Her intense, dark eyes also matched Lewellyn's, with the exception of red blotches surrounding the sockets that hinted of unrelenting tears.

She was wearing black jeans and a soft black turtleneck sweater that set off the healthy glow of her skin. In spite of the blotches around her eyes and a nose reddened from sniffles, Osborne found her to be a very attractive young woman.

"Doc, you've met Suzanne, haven't you?" asked Lew, stepping back from their embrace.

"Last summer, briefly. Good to see you again, Suzanne. How are you doing? How was your drive?" Osborne set down the bread knife and extended his hand in welcome only to realize he had just said the wrong thing.

"O-o-o-h, M-o-o-m-m-m," Suzanne wept. She dropped her overnight bag onto the floor next to the kitchen table before burying her face in her mother's shoulder. "I'm not ... I'm not ..." She mumbled into Lew's shirt.

"All right, hon, let's step into the other room for a minute," said Lew, patting her back.

Lew had warned Osborne to expect some drama: "But I want her to get over feeling sorry for herself. She's done many things right in her life—but if her husband wants to leave and refuses counseling ... Well, she needs realize you can't change other people so get over it. I survived under worse circumstances so I know she can."

"Easy to say, Lew, but I remember trying to help Mallory when she was going through her divorce. Nothing I said seemed to work."

"I know, I know," Lew had said with a heavy sigh. "I'm just hoping Suzanne can find herself a good therapist and a good lawyer: just be a good businesswoman and get through this with no bitterness. She's got a well-paying job that she likes and two lovely children, she ought to be able to manage this."

While the two women commiserated in Lew's bedroom, Osborne finished buttering the bread, checked the pasta water to see if it was boiling yet and was happy to hear Ray stamping his feet out on the porch.

"Yo!" called a familiar voice, "anybody home? Whoa, smells like an Italian whorehouse in here. Need bread for that garlic?"

"Hurry on in and close the door," said Osborne, feeling a rush of icy air as Ray poked his head into the kitchen. "Lew's daughter, Suzanne, just got here. She's in with her mother for a few minutes. Why don't you hang your jacket on the porch and we'll wait for the ladies."

"Ladies with a plural? I like the sound of *that*." Ray's good spirits were a relief. He looked good, too, in a cable-knit Irish sweater the color of oatmeal and comfortably worn dark brown corduroy pants. Losing the trademark beard may not have been a bad thing as his well-shaven face emphasized his strong features and the humor in his light brown eyes.

Ray ambled over to the counter just as Lew and Suzanne returned to the kitchen. There was a moment of silence but before Osborne could open his mouth to make the introductions, Suzanne had spun around to run back towards the bedroom.

"I think she wants to freshen up a bit," said Lew with a wink. Sure enough, minutes later Suzanne reappeared having worked some magic around her eyes: the red was gone and a nice pink flush colored her cheeks.

"Suzanne, you know Ray Pradt, don't you?" asked Lew. "Weren't you two in high school together?"

"I think you were two years ahead of me," said Suzanne as she shook Ray's hand. "I knew who you are though. We have friends in common. What I remember is you making that final basket to win the state championship. Do you remember me?"

"Umm, I'm not sure," said Ray, studying her face. "I'll bet you've changed since then."

"Jeez, I sure hope so," said Suzanne with a laugh. "I certainly do hope so."

That had to come as a relief to Suzanne, thought Osborne. Lew had told him that right after graduating high school, when the paper mill had laid off workers and jobs were hard to come by in the Northwoods, to earn money for college Suzanne worked a summer as a stripper and waitress at the notorious Thunder Bay Bar. It was a job that paid well but did little for a girl's reputation.

"Ray's had a bad week, too," said Lew, dumping handfuls of linguine into the pot of boiling water. "Doc and I thought the two of you might do well with a good meal and an easy evening among friends."

Suzanne gave Ray a measured look before furrowing her brow and saying, "So, your marriage is in the toilet, too?"

Lurching back in surprise, Ray said, "Hell, no. I'm not married."

"Then what's your problem?" Suzanne picked up a celery stick and crunched it between her teeth. Osborne could be mistaken but she seemed to have brightened up since returning to the kitchen.

"I'd rather not discuss it," said Ray. "Just a … bad … week."

"Oh, okay," said Suzanne.

"Tell you what, you two," said Lew, "Doc and I need space here in the kitchen. So why don't you help yourselves to something cold from the fridge and go chat in the living room until dinner is ready."

What Lew called a "living room" was less a room than a nook: a small but warm and cozy area right beside the kitchen that held an old oak-framed leather sofa, one Mission-style rocker and a gas fireplace at the far end. Colorful rag rugs were scattered across the wood floor.

Following her mother's suggestion, Suzanne reached into the fridge for a beer and stepped back to let Ray choose a drink. He, too, reached for a beer. Suzanne gave him a funny look then led the way to the next room.

"So, c'mon, tell me what's haywire in *your* world," she said as they sat side by side on the leather sofa, "I might enjoy having a partner in misery."

Lew and Doc locked eyes, eyebrows raised. Apparently they would have no difficulty overhearing the conversation.

"No big deal," said Ray. "I just … I didn't get a job that I'm perfect for is all. I'm thirty-two, I've been working my ass off, I have no health insurance, no retirement and now no job. That's all."

"I see. And so why did you get that beer?"

"What difference is it to you?"

"I said I knew who you are. And I have certainly heard about your drinking. You dated Ashley Smith a few years ago—she's a good friend of mine. She and I had lunch recently and she said she heard you've been recovering, going to AA and stuff. She'd like to hear from you, you know."

"That's not what I asked you," said Ray. "I asked what the hell you care if I have a beer or not. You don't know me."

"No, I don't. But I grew up with a dad who drank and it's no fun. Thanks to booze, my brother ended up dead after a bar fight. You may be thirty-two with no job but you look great and—"

"I do not need a lecture."

"Sorry." She didn't sound sorry. Osborne glanced over at Lew who was busy dressing the salad and did not look up.

"As far as this beer goes, I have it to *look at.* That's all. I do that sometimes. I test myself." Lew gave Osborne a quizzical look to which he responded with an affirmative nod. Ray had been known to keep a can of beer in his refrigerator for exactly the same reason.

"Really," Suzanne sounded doubtful.

"Just watch. How long you in town?"

"The weekend. Got the news my husband wants a divorce three days ago. Turns out he's been bopping the bookkeeper at the real estate agency where he works so I left our two kids with friends and thought I'd hide out here for a few days. Think things over. Decide what to do next," she said with a sigh.

"So you criticize my beer and here you are—running away. How smart is that?"

"Give me a break, will you? I have to go back and deal with the jerk so I'm not *exactly* running away."

There was silence for a few seconds, then Ray said, "You must have known he was an asshole when you married him."

"Yeah, well hope springs eternal, doncha know," said Suzanne with a light laugh. "I know things will work out. I mean, look at my mom." This time when Osborne glanced over at Lew, he thought he saw a tear glisten in her eye.

"You're a very attractive woman and I can tell you're smart," said Ray. "Why would he leave you?"

"Good question. I had my first visit with a therapist yesterday and I guess one thing might be that I've had more success than he has. I've done well as a CPA—make three times what he does. And there's a lot we don't do together. I run and work out while he's allergic to fresh air. I like movies, he's big on TV sports. That might be part of it. Plus we married pretty young. Ten years ago." She paused, then said, "the weird thing is the bookkeeper looks like his mother—maybe that's it."

"You're kidding!" Ray chuckled. "She looks like his *mother?*"

"I'm not making that up. Hand me your beer, please. I finished mine."

Ray must have held his back as he said, "Hold on now, you're not honoring a family tradition, are you?"

"Hey, if I have one glass of wine or a bottle of beer a week, that's a lot for me. Tonight I feel like I'm coming out from under a goddamn cloud of stress and two beers won't kill me. Not like I'm driving anywhere."

"Okay, here. What are you doing tomorrow night? Want to go out for dinner?"

"I'm married."

"Kind of. I've dated married ladies." On hearing that Osborne rolled his eyes at Lew.

"So I've heard. And I've heard plenty about you, Ray Pradt." Suzanne laughed and then said, "Sure, okay."

"Dinner is ready," Lew called out from where she had just set a large bowl of pasta on the table.

She grinned at Osborne who whispered, "Good work, you. We're about to have dinner with two people who haven't felt this good in days. Even makes me happy."

Beaming, Lew gave him a quick peck on the cheek.

Chapter 17

"So, Ray," said Osborne as they were passing their plates around the table for Lew to serve everyone from the bowl of pasta, "were you able to check out Gina's cabin okay?"

"Oh yeah. Remember the power outage we had during the last ice storm? For some reason, maybe a power surge, almost all her appliances were on including the television and the DVD player—and the heat, too. I called to tell her I turned everything off but left the heat on low so her water pipes don't freeze. Nothing was damaged."

"Good" said Lew. "Thanks for handling all that, Ray. We'll be on a conference call with Gina tomorrow trying to figure out the computer crisis at the tech college. Based on what we've told her, she seems to think it won't take long to figure out who the culprit is. I sure hope she's right so we can concentrate on the Beltner case."

"What's that, Mom?" Suzanne gave her mother a quizzical look.

"Oh golly, would you mind if we talked about that later?" asked Lew. "It's a sad, frustrating case that doesn't make for the best dinner conversation."

"By the way," said Ray, in a light tone of voice, "late this afternoon I stopped into the Loon Lake Market for some mouse traps for Gina's cabin and one of the clerks there said he heard the fishing teams from all the foreign countries should be in town by tomorrow afternoon."

"The teams and a couple thousand tourists, not to mention media from across the country," said Lew, as she passed the salad to Suzanne. "You wouldn't believe how many requests for security we've had to turn down. People must think the Loon Lake police and sheriff's departments have nothing to do except to watch over their equipment." She shook her head.

"Where are they from? This is an *international* fishing tournament?" asked Suzanne. "Here in Loon Lake? Wow, Mom, that's exciting."

"It sure is. For Loon Lake, it's the equivalent of hosting the Olympics. I'm just hoping everything stays calm," said Lew. "Let fish get caught, let TV crews do their thing and, please God, let no vehicles go through the ice.

"The good news is that the tournament is only a week long and it does bring in a lot of tourists, which works for everyone. There'll be a dance and an ice shanty contest. Vendors are setting up in the high school gym—"

"And there's a reality TV show starting to shoot, too," said Ray in a non-committal tone.

"Wow, that's amazing," said Suzanne. "Maybe I'll come back later in the week."

As the conversation buzzed, Osborne basked in the warmth of the voices, the aromas from the dinner table, the glow of friendship on the faces of the people around him. No wonder young people like Suzanne and Ray—even older folks like himself and Lew—don't want to be alone. Does anyone?

After Osborne and Ray had cleared the table and washed the dinner dishes, Ray started towards the door. "See you folks tomorrow," he said, then paused and walked into the living room where the two women were chatting. "Suzanne, you want to go for a ride?"

"Sure." Suzanne jumped up from where she had been sitting on the sofa with her legs tucked under her. "Where we going?"

"Few miles down the highway to the Merriman ski trails. Doc, ever since you asked me if anyone lives in the swamp that runs along the west loop of the Merriman Ski Trails, I've been thinking. I know I've seen deer stands in there but whether anybody actually *lives* in there? Tell the truth—I'm really not sure. So I got hold of some logging maps today and marked a couple lanes that if the snow isn't too deep, I'll go check 'em out."

"Tonight?" asked Lew. "Don't push it, Ray. I'd hate for you to get stuck in there. You know cell service is spotty once you're off the main roads. Suzanne, if you go—dress warm. I wouldn't trust the heat in Ray's truck."

"I wouldn't trust Ray's truck, period," said Osborne. "Lew's right, Ray. That may not be such a great idea."

"Hey, it's not even nine o'clock yet and I figure if anyone is living back in there, I might see lights. Give me an idea where to look in the daylight. And, Chief, don't worry—I'm not driving the lanes tonight. Just the county road that loops around the swamp along the west side and down across the far end."

"All right, Ray," said Lew, reluctance in her voice. "But if you see anything, you wait to follow it up tomorrow, promise? I never trust people who live with no fire numbers. Those are the ones who eat their young."

"Chief, I hear you. I will not put your daughter at risk."

"We'll see about *that*," said Suzanne with an easy grin. She was definitely happier than when she had arrived. And so was Ray.

"Okay, Doc, ready for Session Twenty-One?" asked Lew after the door had closed behind Ray and Suzanne.

"Sure," said Osborne, taking his spot on the sofa with pen and notebook in hand while Lew inserted the DVD they had been working their way through since the holidays. *Joan Wulff's Dynamics of Fly Casting* was Osborne's winter assignment: to watch and practice the basics of fly fishing as demonstrated by one of the icons in the sport. Their pattern had been to watch a session or two on the evenings he spent at her place. While watching, Osborne often found himself taking notes to carry with him later when the season opened.

Jotting down tips on the power snap, loading line, changing direction while casting, and shooting line had already filled more than a few pages. Worried at first that it would be too technical for a beginner like himself, Osborne found himself enjoying the video more than he had expected. Joan Wulff made fly casting look easy as she broke the movements down into simple steps that were definitely less intimidating than the books he had tried to read.

Maybe he also liked it because watching Joan Wulff's rhythmic motions as she demonstrated technique reminded him of Lew's grace in the water—especially in the moonlight on warm summer evenings. Instructions and nice memories: not a bad way to end a long winter's day.

"Here's where it gets fun," said Lew as she hit the remote buttons and Session Twenty-One came up on the screen. "The double haul. Doc, when you can double haul—I'll buy dinner."

"Deal," said Osborne, nestling in beside her on the sofa. The video started to run and he watched dumbfounded as Joan Wulff's hands moved in opposite directions. "Lewellyn, excuse me, would you back that up, please?"

Osborne leaned forward to watch closely. "Um, back it up again, please?" After the fourth viewing, he said, "Is this where they separate the men from the boys?"

Lew laughed. "You'll get the hang of it. Just takes practice. All you need is to remember the haul is fast and the give back is slow."

"That's not what worries me. It's both hands moving in opposite directions. I have enough trouble tying on a Size 18 dry fly without tackling this. How 'bout I just false cast for the rest of my life?"

"Doc, I said I'd buy dinner ..."

"Yeah, that's one safe bet. This looks very confusing. Let's go back and watch the section on casting into a headwind. I can master that. I like the part about not worrying over the presentation of your dry fly because the water is so choppy—"

Just then the back door opened and Suzanne came in.

"Back so soon?" said Lew, hitting the Pause button.

"You bet—it is cold out there. I got so chilly—I don't think that truck has any heat. Man, my feet are frozen!"

"See anything?" asked Lew.

"Maybe. We drove around the swamp area as far as the road would allow. We saw lights in three different locations—though Ray thought we might have been seeing the headlights of other cars. Dr. Osborne, he said he would call you tomorrow to see if you've got time to go with him and check those out."

"He wants my car is what he wants," said Osborne, getting up from the sofa. "A vehicle with heat. Lewellyn, it is time for me to head home. Thank you for a wonderful meal and, Suzanne, nice seeing you again.

"Hope this visit is therapeutic. I told your mom that my oldest daughter had a similar experience a few years ago. Her husband took up with her best friend. She's since finished grad school, landed a great job, loves her apartment, loves living in Chicago. I know she would tell you the divorce was the best thing that could have happened given how her life has changed."

He left out the part about Mallory having a brief fling with Ray Pradt. A fling that had been good for her ego even if it had given Osborne heartburn; Ray was someone he valued as a friend but not the best candidate for a son-in-law. The good news was both parties were now just friends.

"I'm off to a good start thanks to you and Mom tonight. That Ray is fun to be around." Suzanne shook her head as she grinned, "You know, he is just plain cute."

As she walked Osborne to the door, Lew gave him a quick kiss and a smile that radiated satisfaction. Ray Pradt had certainly boosted Suzanne's spirits and, it appeared, she may have done the same for him. Mission accomplished.

"Doc, before you go to sleep tonight take a few minutes to practice that double haul exercise in the mirror—the one where you swing your body from side to side while using your line hand to haul as you swing."

"Sounds like a recipe for a nightmare, Lewellyn. Thank you."

Once in his car, he found he had a message from Ray on his cell phone: "Doc, that swamp isn't as empty as I thought. What are you doing tomorrow morning right after daylight? That would give us time to see what might be back there. Then maybe I could borrow your car later to pick up Suzanne?"

Osborne chuckled. Yep, Ray sounded like his old self.

CHAPTER 18

It was just twelve noon on Sunday morning. Beth Hellenbrand, head of the computer technology department, had taken a seat between Osborne and Lew in the Office of the President at the college. Lew had stressed with Patience that the only individual capable of taking the highly technical directions via phone calls and emails likely to come from Gina would be an experienced computer programmer. Beth was elected.

A slim woman of medium height, Beth Hellenbrand had the narrow skull, high checkbones and firm jaw of her Swedish ancestors. As she had entered the room, Osborne was struck by the simple lines of her face, which reflected the small-boned structure of her entire body. Quite a contrast to Patience.

Her manner was solemn—she had yet to break a smile—and the intelligence in her eyes, which were the crystalline blue of a lake under a summer sun and a cloudless sky, signaled that she felt in command when it came to computer technology. But she was so serious that Osborne began to wonder if she was angry about something.

"My degree is in computer engineering," Beth was saying in quiet voice after being introduced to Lew and Osborne, "after which I spent two years working with the eBay tech teams in northern California before I moved back here to take this job.

Just so you know, I have made some progress on following the trail of the spammer so far. We have been able to set up so we can at least see exactly when they enter our system."

As she spoke, she opened the briefcase she had carried in and pulled out a laptop computer, which she set unopened on her lap.

"Do you think it is one or several of our students doing this?" asked Patience from where she sat behind her desk. Osborne and Lew had set their chairs in a semi-circle, one on each side of Beth, as the four of them waited for Gina to call in on the speakerphone.

"That would mean one of my students," said Beth. "I find that difficult to believe because I know each one quite well. They are hard-working kids. But at the suggestion of an old friend from school, I did do a tour of the parking lot to see if anyone is driving a new, expensive car. Students who make money off hacking and identity theft are often dumb enough to go out and buy themselves fancy SUVs or sports cars."

"Any luck?" interrupted Patience.

"No," said Beth, "and that, frankly was a relief."

The phone rang. It was Gina, sounding as always like she was ready to give orders and chop off heads. "Got your laptop running?" she asked Beth once they were introduced.

"Yes, ready." Beth did not appear in the least intimidated. Her fingers danced across the keyboard as Gina clarified what she knew so far—she'd had the morning to explore the tech college system remotely. Then Gina was quiet and everyone waited.

"Here's the thing," said Gina, "given what you folks have told me, what my grad students know and what we have been able to track on the monitors, we aren't the right people to help you."

Beth's head perked up even as Patience's shoulders slumped. Worry crossed Lew's face. Gina continued, "We are database investigators and you need someone with expertise in digital forensics." Beth nodded in silent agreement.

"Where do we find someone like that?" asked Patience. "Is this going to take forever?" Her voice cracked as if she would break into tears.

"Hell, no," said Gina. "I got the right person all lined up. Can you take another caller on your line there? Do you have conference mode?"

"Hold on," said Patience, "I'll take care of it just bear with me for a moment."

Bustling over to the door ask her secretary for instructions, Patience reminded Osborne of a fluffed up mother hen leaning over a tiny chick: a stark difference he would find humorous if she didn't look so frazzled. The bags under her eyes testified to a sleepless night and when she sat back down at the desk, her hands shook as she pressed the phone console to reach the college operator.

"We're ready for the call," said Patience, "please go ahead."

"Great," said Gina, her voice strong over the speakerphone. "Everyone, I'd like to run this problem by a good friend and former colleague, Julie Davis, who is consulting for companies like Google and Microsoft on security issues and identity theft— she works in northern California."

"Ouch," said Lew, "a consultant? How much will this cost us? Patience, can the college afford another consultant?"

"Hold on," said Gina, before Patience could answer, "Money is not an issue. Julie owes me. I just did some database investigative work for one of her clients—pro bono. Plus my bet is she can knock this one out in less than five minutes ..." After a brief pause, Osborne heard the ping of another phone line patched through to the office. "Hello, Julie?"

"Hey, Gina, what's up?" asked a bright voice through the speakerphone. Even though they could hear easily, everyone in the room leaned forward in their chairs. After a round of introductions, Gina quickly laid out the situation, starting with the strange behavior of the computer in Patience's home office to the inundation of the college network with spam messages.

"Okay, got it," said Julie. I worked with UC Santa Cruz on a similar problem last year. You have work to do, folks, and, yes, the Feds are right: it could very well be a student or students on your campus. But this sounds sophisticated enough that I'll need a good tech on your end who can take orders from me."

"That would be me," said Beth. "Beth Hellenbrand, I run the computer department here."

"And I may be able to help some," said Gina, "but Beth is on site and she's got a degree in computer engineering."

"Great," said Julie. "You know code, Beth?"

"I'm good at solving puzzles," said Beth. "Yes, I know code though it hasn't been much help yet."

"But you are very familiar with the system there—hardware *and* software?"

"Yes."

"What about back-up. You'll want two people on this—it may require twenty-four hour monitoring of the system."

"I know just the person," said Beth, her voice firm as she leaned towards the speakerphone, "one of my students, Danielle. I'll see if I can't get her in here right now. Excuse me while I have her paged."

"Take your time," said Julie, "no rush on this end. Beth set her laptop down and walked out of the office. While she was gone, Julie said in a chatty tone, "You caught me at a good time, Gina. I fly up to the Microsoft campus later today. So you're working in Wisconsin?"

"Not here at the tech college. I'm still down south at the university. Initially I thought my team and I could help out here but our hacking skills didn't get us far. All we could get was a bunch of spam return addresses already canceled. There has to be a trick to this that we don't know. By the way, Julie, part of the problem— a big part of the problem—is that the spam messaging appears to come from Dr. Schumacher herself and from her personal laptop."

"I'm not surprised," said Julie as the office door opened and Beth returned.

"Danielle will be right over. She's leaving a class," said Beth picking up her laptop.

"Good," said Julie. "While we wait, let me give you an idea of what you are dealing with. The easiest way to describe it is this: someone, likely a student, has hacked into your system and opened a pipeline for spammers. More than one from the sound of it, which is not unusual. The spammer pays for access based on the number of email addresses made available. By the way, have you had complaints from any other schools?"

"Yes," said a breathy female voice from behind Osborne. "Professor Hellenbrand, I didn't have a chance to tell you but down in IT we got calls from twenty-seven different tech schools over the weekend. Their networks are overwhelmed with spam and they've traced it to us."

The voice belonged to a young woman with a round sweet face set that seemed to hang in a cloud of dangling brunette ringlets. Osborne couldn't help but see her as three spheres stacked one upon the other: her pale, moon face centered over a rotund torso balanced in turn on a too-generous rear end. An attempt had been made to camouflage the spheres under a flattering maroon sweater and roomy black sweatpants.

"Ouch, that is *not* what I was hoping to hear," said Julie. "All right, is everyone sitting down?"

As if she could hear them, everyone in the room nodded their heads. "Based on my experience, it would seem your hacker has access to the networks connecting other technical colleges to your campus. How that can happen is information that authorities keep in strictest confidence, but I *can* tell you that your network at the college may be the source of spam going out to several *hundred* schools."

Beth turned around to Danielle who had taken a chair at the back of the room. "Give me an idea of what schools we have complaints from."

"Sure," said Danielle looking down at a notepad in her lap, "we had calls from tech schools in Minnesota, Michigan, Illinois, Nebraska—"

"That's enough," said Julie, "I'm sure they're into the entire tech college network— possibly over a thousand schools. You'll be hearing from more as they figure it out.

"Here's the real danger: because the messages appear to be sent from the schools— or, more specifically, from senior level staff like yourself, Dr. Schumacher—there is a high level of trust in the message. Because of this connection, students are more likely to believe a fraudulent message or click on a dubious link.

"Worse yet, that willingness to respond often allows the criminals—and the spammers are criminals, believe me—to mine student responses for personal information such as birth dates, addresses, phone numbers—all the tidbits that can be used in identity theft. Once they have the name and email address, they can go on Facebook or some other social networking site and pluck whatever additional information they need."

"Oh my God," said Patience, "will we be sued?"

"Not if you can prove your school is a victim, too. But you have to find the hacker perpetrating this and that may not be easy. Beth, Danielle, Gina—what are you up to late this afternoon?"

"I'm here until five thirty," said Beth, "I have to leave then."

"I'm available," said Danielle, "I can skip class. If you want, I can work until ten or eleven tonight, too. Call me Dani by the way—I mean, that's what I go by."

"You have classes on Sundays?" asked Julie.

"Yes," said Patience. "We have many students with full-time jobs during the week so we offer a full weekend program."

"Okay," said Julie, "let me email you in a few minutes, Beth—tell me your email. I have to check with my client to see how long our meeting will take this afternoon and then we'll get right on this."

"How long do you think it will take to locate the source of this spam?" asked Patience. "I am so worried that students may respond to offers like huge discounts on smartphones and the textbooks. I have talked with several of our students who responded right away to some of the original spam. They all want smartphones and these crooks, whoever they are, know just how to tap into that temptation for new technology."

"I wish I could give you an answer on how quickly we can pinpoint the person or persons behind the spamming," said Julie. "From the sound of it, Dr. Schumacher, once I have a chance to get a closer look at the situation with Beth and her assistant we'll have a much better sense of what we're up against. Meanwhile have your staff get alerts out to all the tech schools on the network ASAP."

"Right."

"Don't forget to alert your own student body, too. Tell them not to click on any links or even consider any of these tantalizing offers they're getting in their email, especially if the offer appears to come from your office or the college."

"Got it. Beth and Dani will help me with this," said Patience.

"Jeez Louise," said Lew once Julie was off the speakerphone. "Wow. Looks like have our hands full, folks."

"Beth," said Patience, rubbing a weary hand across her brow, "how much should the school pay Dani for her time?"

"Ten dollars an hour is the usual," said Beth, "but Dr. Schumacher, let's double that. She may be working through the night."

"Fine," said Patience. "I'll pay out of my own pocket if I have to. This is frightening. What if we can't stop—"

"What's your major, Dani?" asked Lew. "Are you working on a two-year degree in computer science here then going onto the university?"

"Cosmetology."

"*Cosmetology?*" Lew looked horrified and Beth stifled a smile.

"Oh," said Danielle with a shy smile as she rocked slightly in her chair, "I do this stuff for fun. My mom's a hairdresser—so that's kinda what I wanna be, too."

"Well, just wait and see, kid," said Lew. "This project may change your life. Don't you find all this a little more exciting than ... cosmetology?"

"Um, kinda," said Dani with a shrug and a nervous glance at Patience, "but I'm on a cosmetology scholarship?" Her voice lifted with a note of uncertainty as though worried she might offend someone.

"Now hold on," said Patience, getting up from her chair and walking over to drape a protective arm around Danielle's shoulders. "Dani has made a good choice for her career. Loon Lake needs stylists as much as computer techs.

"Dani is my poster child for why Wheedon College offers two-year degrees in cosmetology, nursing, early childhood education and the culinary arts along with the building trades. She grew up here, she wants to start a family here—right, Dani?" Danielle nodded meekly.

It struck Osborne that if Patience Schumacher lacked self-confidence around accomplished adults, she was the opposite around the tech college students—possibly insufferable.

"We groom our students to make a good living in all the services required in communities like Loon Lake, like Rhinelander, like Minocqua. Cosmetology is as necessary as plumbing—at least that was my father's philosophy when he endowed the college."

Osborne recalled the referendum vote ten years earlier when the county residents had voted against establishing a technical college. Local taxpayers, especially those in the rural areas, felt they would be overwhelmed with the costs.

Immediately after the defeat, Patience Schumacher's father had stepped forward with the plan and the funding to launch the college. He had one stipulation: the family trust would pay for the building of the campus and operating costs for ten years so long as the country board agreed to allow his daughter, Patience, to chair the administration and manage the funding from the Schumacher Trust over that same period of time.

Before leaving the office with Dani in tow, Beth said, "Chief Ferris, I'm afraid I cannot put in unlimited time on this. I have four young children and a husband who also has a full time job as an engineer—so I'll be asking Dani to handle the late hours.

"Also, I lost a very close friend this week, and I'm helping her husband with the family and the funeral service. They are devastated. I have to be there."

"Do you mind if I ask who you are referring to?" asked Lew. "Someone local, I take it?"

"Kathy Beltner, the wife of my husband's partner and one of my closest friends. Rob Beltner and my husband, Bart, run Krist Engineering and—"

"Look, Beth," said Lew, "you take the time you need to. I'll plan to handle any surveillance required here at the college. If Dani has to work late, I will be here, too."

CHAPTER 19

At two thirty that Sunday afternoon, and then only after leaving three voicemail messages of increasing urgency, Osborne was able to reclaim his car, which Ray had asked to borrow while Osborne was wolfing down a late lunch. His excuse was he had offered to drive an elderly widow living down the road from them to a church gathering. That was over an hour and a half ago.

When the car finally arrived, it contained an unapologetic driver and a Ziploc of half-frozen fresh-caught crappies on the passenger seat.

"I wish you had told me you were going fishing," said Osborne, irritated.

"Was only out for about an hour," said Ray as if time was the issue rather than the hijacking of someone else's vehicle. "Plus ... I had research to undertake and *that* ... had to be undertaken in strictest confidence."

"Research? Research for what?"

Ray put a finger to his lips. "Sworn to secrecy, sorry. So hey, Doc, okay with you if we buzz out to the swamp and check it out? Do our best to be back by four? I'll be needing to shower and get ready to pick up Suzanne—"

"Why don't you just follow me in your truck? In that case, should we run late you can take off whenever you want to."

"Nah. This'll be fine." Osborne had suggested the other only to tease his neighbor. The current temperature was twenty below zero and that was not counting the wind chill. If anything in Ray's world could be relied upon that day, it would be the heat in Osborne's Subaru.

They parked near the first spot where Ray thought he had seen lights and discovered a snowmobile trail running parallel to the road. A swift walk along the trail brought them to an intersection where two trails crossed. The snow was packed down, indicating a number of snowmobiles had been parked there. A well-trodden path led to a clearing where they found the remains of a party: smashed beer cans, cigarette butts, crumpled popcorn and potato chip bags as well as a scattering of blackened stumps left from a bonfire.

"Okay, so much for this place," said Ray. He checked a page that had been torn from a Gazetteer and overlaid with hand-drawn sketches of logging lanes. "Got Butch Day to show me these," he said, scanning the map. "Okay." Ray shoved the map into his jacket pocket. "Let's drive down past Wind Pudding Road and see what we see."

Just past Wind Pudding, Ray motioned for Osborne to pull into a snowy lane that had not seen a plow in weeks. "Not sure about this," said Osborne, "four-wheel drive can only take us so far. We'd be wise to walk in. Either that or you'll be late for your date because we'll be digging ourselves out of here."

"Walking works for me," said Ray, opening the car door. They trudged ahead, pushing through the shin-shearing crust over snow so deep it spilled into the tops of their boots. It was hard going.

Ten minutes into the workout, Osborne balked. "You sure about this? I am not having fun. Wish we had those snowshoes, darn. Too bad we left those in your truck."

"Hang in there, Doc," said Ray, plunging through the snow twenty feet ahead of Osborne. "Hey! Got somebody living back here …"

Coming around a bend in the lane, Osborne glimpsed a small dark green shack not unlike hundreds of others left over from the region's heydays of logging in the late 1800s and early 1900s. As they got closer he could see a lean-to attached to the shed. Inside the lean-to was a pile of plastic gallon jugs and parked next to the lean-to was a rusted-out pick-up that hinted at once being bright red. That it still ran was evident from tire tracks in the snow. The tracks lead off in the opposite direction.

"Jeez," said Osborne, "there *is* a road in here—and plowed to boot. Too bad we didn't know that."

Ray was already knocking on the door of the shack. After a few knocks, the stained metal knob on the door rattled for a few seconds until the mechanism caught and the door was opened by the bent figure of a man who looked to be at least a hundred years old. He was dressed in heavy grey wool hunting pants held up with black suspenders and a red and black checked wool shirt. He was bald and his eyes bleary.

"Walter Frisch!" said Ray, stepping back in surprise. "What the hell you doing way out here?"

"Oh," the old man leaned forward to squint at him then chewed his gums for a moment before continuing, "oh, hi there. So it's you, Ray?" He peered past Ray and Osborne was going to be surprised if the old guy could see more than a shadow. "Got somebody there with you? Come on in and warm up."

"Don't mind if I do. Doc, you know old Walter—he's the hermit used to live up on Shepard Lake road. When'd you move out here, Walt?"

"My niece inherited that property from my sister and after Sis died, well, she kicked me off. Wants to develop the place. Take a seat over there, you two."

Walter waved a hand indicating the two of them should sit on a sagging daybed wedged into one corner of the one room shack. The entire room could not be much more than eight by ten feet. Tiny. Tiny, but warm and cozy and lit with two kerosene lamps, the glow from which made Walter's bald head shine. Glancing around the room Osborne noticed it was sparsely furnished with neatly stacked belongings that included a few canned goods and boxes of other foodstuffs. A gallon jug of water was set under a small table in one corner that also held a miniature portable television set.

Osborne recalled random sightings of the old hermit over the years, Walter walking or running along the strange fence line he had created along Shepard Lake Road, saplings he bent and tied in odd patterns. In time Walter became a Loon Lake phenomenon, and people took visitors to see their own home-grown folk artist of sorts.

More than one parent made it a practice to take Sunday afternoon drives along Shepard Lake Road and point out Walter's peculiar sculptures to wide-eyed children with the warning: "that's what you'll be doing if you don't keep your grades up ..." A warning that had had a significant effect on Osborne's youngest daughter.

Not long after he had intoned the dire future that might lie ahead for any child scoring a C or worse at school, Erin had run home with her third grade report card. Refusing to go out and play, she had waited for her father to get home from the dental office. Then, with eyes so serious he had to look away to avoid smiling, she had shown him the card filled with straight A's and said as only a worried child can: "So now I don't have to grow up and be a hermit—right, Dad?"

"Yep, yep, when my niece kicked me off I remembered this place from when I was a kid and we hunted frogs out here," Walter was saying. "Look," he banged on the wall, "solid oak and no holes for the wind to come through. Some logger built it and lived here 'round nineteen hun'erd, I'll betcha.

"Got my propane heater there, use the outdoors for a refrigerator, got my battery-powered TV. Got an outhouse out back. Yep, yep, livin' off my military pension and most days I drive in to eat at Wal-Mart in that diner. They got good specials, y'know."

"But," Ray looked around the place before saying, "how do you get your pension check? You can't get mail out here. You don't have a fire number."

"Don't need a fire number to get a post office box. Say, I know this don't look like much but I like it. Hey, I even got HBO— one of my nephews felt sorry when his sister kicked me off the property. He rigged it up for me to get it off the satellite somehow."

As Walter spoke, he scuttled quickly across the room to pull out the one remaining chair—a kitchen chair with a yellow vinyl seat torn down the middle—and sat down. He leaned towards them as he talked. Every word seemed to require a lengthy working of his jaw so Osborne didn't want to put him out too much.

"Know of anyone else living back in here?" asked Osborne. "I can't imagine you see too many people with all this wetland around ..."

"Oh," Walter said, gumming away, "there's plenty high ground. Summertime your boots might get a little wet, yeah, and the mosquitoes are bad, but plenty high ground if you know where to look. Why, you fellas looking to start a *homes association*? Heh, heh." Walter laughed at his own joke. The eyes could barely see, the body could not straighten up, but he had not lost his sense of humor.

"Walter, Doc Osborne and I are working with the Loon Lake Police. A woman was found shot to death over on the Merriman Trails. Any chance you've heard anything about that?"

"No-o-o, I don't believe I have. Hear lots of gunshots though," said the old man. "Got a fella took over that camp where the Russians used to hang out, y'know? And he's always shooting. Going after rabbits is what he told me."

"You shoot rabbits?" asked Ray.

"Me? Hell, I haven't had the strength to lift a rifle for years now. Nope, but I sure wish I could—"

"*The Russian camp?* Gosh, I forgot all about that place," said Osborne, turning to Ray. "You know what Walter is talking about?"

"Nope."

"Well, when I was a kid, I used to play with a friend whose family had a farm about a mile from here. My friend and I would walk up to the swamp and we knew a path that ran in a ways to a spot where we could hide and watch these old Russians who lived in a cabin out here. Who knows if they really were Russian but there were five or six men and everyone just called them 'those old Russians.'

"Doesn't take much to intrigue little kids so my buddy and I would hide out and watch them chopping wood, carrying their water. Yeah, I know that place but I don't know if I could find it today."

"Hmm, yeah, I'll show ya," said Walter. "It still ain't easy to find. You take my road out and when you get to the fork, you go past a ways and on your right you'll see a big hemlock got hit by lightning. Just past that you'll see a logging lane, take that in a quarter mile to where it forks and you take the lane to your right."

"Oh sure," said Osborne. "I remember the fork. Boy, in my day that was not a drivable road."

"Ha," said Walter, "you can drive it now. Guy who's rebuilding that place takes a truck and an ATV in there. If that's where you're heading, be careful when you go in. He tried to make rabbit stew out of me when I was going by one day. Don't scare me none. He's a squatter just like me—I'll go where I wanna go—and I walk every day, y'know. Keeps me young."

"Walter? How the hell old are you?" asked Ray.

"Ninety-two," said the old man, his eyes crinkling with satisfaction.

"You cook out here ever?" asked Ray, jumping to his feet.

"Yep, yep, got myself a little grill out behind the shack here. Works fine. Why?"

"Doc, you stay here with Walter and I'll be right back."

"Okay," said Osborne, "while you're at the car, figure out how we can find our way over to Lumen Lane. Too cold to risk getting lost."

In less than five minutes, Ray was back with his Ziploc of crappies. "Walter, you are a gentleman and a scholar and I want you to have these. Fresh caught at lunchtime. Got some butter or oil to cook 'em in?" Osborne got to his feet as they talked.

"Yep, yep. Okay, fellas, you come back any time now."   .

"You're pretty friendly for an old hermit," said Ray.

"Never said I didn't like visitors. People seemed to like to keep their distance on their own for some reason and that was okay. When a few of 'em did stop—mostly young boys on bikes like Ray here, well, it was nice to chat. But I understand folks not understanding someone like me.

"Had plenty of time for myself in those days. Took a while to recover from the war, y'know." He looked like he was about to go off on a long tangent and Osborne was anxious to get back to their search before the sun set.

"Well, Walter, if you see or hear anything you think we should know about, drop by the police station and leave me a note. Ask the woman on the switchboard to call Dr. Osborne and she'll know how to reach me."

"Yep, yep, will do."

"Doc, you ready?" Ray opened the door.

"Where you boys off to now?"

"Looking for the impossible, Walt," said Ray. "The victim was snowshoeing and we're trying to find some sign of where she might have been killed. Or even where she was walking before it happened."

"Snowshoeing? Like on those new metal things they got? Hold on." Walter moved past them and out the door to the lean-to where he reached down. "Found this on the road when I was walking the other day. Is this the kind of thing you're looking for?"

He held up one of Kathy Beltner's red aluminum snowshoes.

"What road was that, Walter?" asked Osborne.

"Right by that hemlock I told you about. Before you reach the logging lane into the Russian camp."

"You see much traffic out here? Skiers? Folks on snowshoes?"

"Loggers mostly. No skiers. Least I haven't seen any."

"Mind if we take this snowshoe with us?" asked Osborne.

"Sure. Happy to help. I'll check with that ATV fella—see if he might have found the other one."

"No, don't do that, Walter," said Osborne. "That's our job. Right, Ray?"

"Okedoke."

CHAPTER 20

"I'm going to stop in off and on to visit that old guy, Doc. He shouldn't be living all alone out here," said Ray, sliding into the passenger seat Osborne's car.

"I'd be careful about that if I were you," said Osborne. "You put someone like Walter Frisch in assisting living or a nursing home and he'll be dead in days. Out here the man may be at risk but he's happy. If I were him, I'd want to die during one of those long walks of his—not sitting in a wheelchair."

"You're right. But I'm worried about him keeping an eye on that guy at the Russian camp. Good thing you told him to mind his own business."

Osborne laughed. "Lew needs all the help she can get but I'm sure she'd draw the line at a ninety-two year old deputy. But, you know, I bet you anything old Walter is watching every step that guy takes. What the hell else does he have to do after breakfast at Wal-Mart?"

"Very interesting he found that snowshoe," said Ray. "We'll have to show it to Rob Beltner, but it has to be his wife's. Funny Walter found only one. And just as strange that he found it so far from the trail. Almost as if it fell off a vehicle."

Osborne nodded in agreement. "Say, I'm curious as to what's happening at the old Russian camp. We have time to swing by that place, don't we?"

Ray checked his watch. "Sure. It's only three-fifteen, Doc."

"Take us ten minutes at the most. God forbid we make you late for Suzanne. Hey, here's where we go straight ..."

Osborne slowed to pass the hemlock that had been shattered by lightning. Sure enough, not far beyond was the logging lane just as Walter had said. Turning right onto the lane, he was relieved to see it was well traveled enough that four-wheel drive would get them in and out okay.

The lane forked and he bore right again, memories of the old Russian camp he had known as a kid vivid in his mind. But the structure they drove up to bore little resemblance to the ancient log cabin he remembered.

Someone had shored up the sagging log walls and the exterior appeared to have been power-washed and re-grouted, giving the cabin a fresh, new look. Telephone and power lines had been run in to the back of the building, too. "Looks like who-ever lives here now has electricity and running water?" asked Osborne. "I shouldn't be so surprised. It's been fifty years since I last saw this place."

"Maybe running water," said Ray. "I can see putting a well in out here but a septic? I doubt that. Not in these wetlands." Sure enough, even as they spoke they caught sight of an outhouse beyond the main cabin.

"The original cabin had a tarpaper roof," said Osborne. "Looks like they've added a modern version of a deer stand up there." He pointed to the rooftop, which now sported a crow's nest lined with windows.

"Wow. Look at that! That's something you don't see that very often but handy, for sure," said Ray. "Lots of deer in this swamp. Let's get out and take a closer look. Nobody's around that I can see though over there," he pointed, "I see ruts from a truck coming and going."

"Isn't it peculiar that with all these improvements there's still no fire number?" asked Osborne. He opened the car door and stepped out, "I think the place is developed enough the tax man would be interested—"

"If he can find it," said Ray. He walked over to the cabin to peer through one of the windows.

"Hold on," said Osborne, "I think I hear someone ..." He looked in the direction of a low rumbling noise to see a beat-up black Dodge pick-up approaching. The truck looked overwhelmed by a shiny new snowmobile that it was carrying in its bed. As the pick-up neared, Osborne could make out a dingy red "Dakota Sport" emblazoned on the driver's side. "Yeah, looks like the guy who's rebuilding the place. Let's have a little chat."

The figure that climbed out of the pick-up was imposing to say the least: as tall or taller than Ray's six feet five inches and well over two hundred pounds, though it was tough to tell as he was wearing insulated overalls and a filthy grey-green parka that hung to his knees. A full, unkempt grey beard under a brown hunter's hat with a long brim and earflaps hid most of his face. Barely visible under the brim of the hat were eyes that were not happy.

"You two don't read?" he said in a thin voice that wheezed as he spoke. "This property is posted."

"It is?" challenged Ray in a calm voice. "I didn't see a posting— last time I was out this direction this was all state land. Where is it posted?"

"Maybe it came down in the wind. Who the hell cares? I said you are trespassing. Get outta here. *Now.*" He started towards them, his height and thickness menacing.

"Whoa, is that an Artic Cat Sno Pro 500 you got in your truck there?" asked Ray, pleasantly ignoring the unspoken threat as he pointed at the back of the truck. "I hear that sled is one helluva racer."

The man stepped in front of the truck, barring the way. "You have a hearing problem too?"

"Hey, wait just a minute, fella," said Ray, putting a hand out defensively. "We're deputies with the Loon Lake Police and we're just here to ask a few questions. Only take a minute or two."

"No questions. Leave."

"You want to answer the questions at the station?" asked Ray. Now he took a step towards the guy. Osborne didn't like the feel of the situation at all but he kept his mouth shut. Ray may have had plenty of experience with razzbonyas like this, but not Osborne. He began to hope they could get back in his car alive.

"What is it?" said the man with a grunt.

"Well, sir, first we'd like your name and the address ..." At Ray's cue, Osborne reached into his jacket pocket for a note-book and pen. The man just stared at Ray.

"Forget it. What else you want?"

Ray exhaled and said, "O-o-o-kay. If you don't want to tell us who you are—"

"Until you tell me why you're here, I see no reason to. Got a badge?"

"Not on me at the moment. We're deputies," said Ray, gesturing towards Osborne. The man threw up his hands and started to walk back to the truck.

"I don't have time for this," he said.

"Have you seen any people snowshoeing or skiing back in here in the last week or so?" asked Osborne. "We're trying to locate a lost person—and one of those aluminum snowshoes, a red one. Seen anything like that lately?"

The man stopped and turned. "Why didn't you say so before? No and no. Look around—does this look like the county fairgrounds? This is the middle of a goddamn swamp. All I see out here are deer and rabbits. Now will you get off my property?"

"Thank you, sir, that's all we needed to know," said Ray. "Sorry to have bothered you." He turned to walk back to Osborne's car, then stopped and pointed off to the left of the cabin. "I see you got a carcass hanging off that pine over there. Somebody forget to tell you deer season ended eight weeks ago?"

"Ray ..." Osborne warned.

As they drove down the lane towards the town road that would take them back to the highway, Ray said, "That was a polite conversation. I'm turning that joker in to the game warden. What ... a commode."

"He worried me," said Osborne. "And he seems familiar. That voice. Does he remind you of anyone?"

"Hell, he's like every other jack pine savage who thinks they're entitled to squat wherever," said Ray. "And after I talk to the game warden, I'm calling the DNR and the Forest Service—get that guy outta there pronto." Ray was quiet for a short morment. "Doc, I know that land is not posted. Our friend is squatting and boy is he *irritating*."

"Lew's right about people with no fire numbers," said Osborne. "Chances are they *do* eat their young." As he turned on to the highway, he asked, "That was the last place where you saw lights, right? Because we should get you back to town."

Before Ray could answer, Osborne's cell phone rang. He took the call then closed the phone. "That was Marlaine on the switchboard. Lew wants me at the Schumacher place—it's been vandalized."

CHAPTER 21

Osborne ran up the front steps onto the porch of the Schumacher house and banged on the door. When no one answered, he pushed his way inside. The living room to his right was dark.

"Hello?" he shouted, standing in the foyer and uncertain which way to go. Just then Patience came walking towards him from the back of the house, unsteady on her feet. As she got closer he could see that her cheeks were tear-streaked and her eyes red and swollen.

Throwing her body onto an armchair, which nearly tipped over as she landed, she shook her head in despair and said, "Things are out of control, Dr. Osborne. I don't know what to do." She gave a weak wave in the direction from where she had just come. "Chief Ferris is back in the den—but it has been destroyed. Just *destroyed*. My personal files ransacked. Our bedroom is a disaster. You won't believe it.

"I tell you," she said, her voice shaking, "some evil, angry people—or person—tore through here. And why? My god, why? The things they did to my beautiful home? Oh, I wish Charles were here." As she buried her head in her hands, Osborne gave her a swift pat on the shoulder and headed for the den.

"Doc? Is that you?" called Lew at the sound of his footsteps. "Go slow coming in here so you don't step on any glass ..."

Osborne entered the den to find Lew standing in the midst of a maelstrom of dumped file folders, strewn papers, torn books and shards of glass from lamps that had been smashed on the floor. The desk was the only bare space in the room and he saw why: Patience Schumacher's laptop computer had been knocked onto the floor and bludgeoned to pieces.

"Lewellyn—" Osborne paused, dumbfounded.

"I know. What a mess, huh. Patience called me about half an hour ago. We think whoever did this had to have been in the house for at least an hour. Certainly not on the premises when she got home, which may have been a good thing."

Gazing around the room, Lew gave a heavy sigh as if the prospect of cleaning up—much less investigating—was too daunting.

"Well, Doc, at least you got here fast and I thank you for that. Roger and Todd are so busy with the tournament that I have no other backup. And, frankly, I don't know where to start except to be sure there is no way anyone touches a thing in here tonight. I want the Wausau boys in on this and, believe me—this is one time when I will not take 'no' for an answer."

"Is anything plugged in?" asked Osborne, looking around. "I'm worried about fire."

"I've checked for that. Unplugged the router and the modem, all the lamps, the computer of course. Even the phone. Boy oh boy, this is one hell of a mess. Hard to tell if someone was searching for something or just into tearing the place up. So far Patience isn't sure if anything was stolen though her personal file cabinet was ransacked—all the contents dumped on the floor over there." She pointed.

"You think one person did this?"

Lew shrugged. "Doc, I have no idea but I am beginning to think this has nothing to do with students from the college.

This is rage, pure unadulterated rage. Wait 'till you see the bedroom. But look here first," she pointed to the damaged computer. "Whoever did it must have taken a sledgehammer—something heavy enough to destroy the hard drive."

Osborne followed her into the master bedroom. Dresser drawers had been pulled out and dumped on the floor. Closet doors stood open and piles of clothing had been strewn in every direction. Even curtains and wooden shades had been ripped from the window casings.

Oddly, on the couple's king-size bed, the bedspread, blankets and sheets had been piled up and left in a teepee-like heap in the middle of the bed. Osborne walked across the room towards the bed.

"Doc, wait," said Lew, handing him a pair of Nitrile gloves, "we don't want to touch a thing here or in the den without gloves on."

"This looks like there might be something hidden under here," said Osborne, studying the strange mound. "A dead animal? Do they have a dog? I don't remember seeing one."

"That's why I called you," said Lew. "I decided I'd just as soon find out what it is with you here." She dropped her voice, "Forget Patience. She is just this side of full-blown hysterics."

"Where's the husband?"

"In Milwaukee taking an art seminar at the university. Supposedly." Lew gave Osborne a knowing look. "Due back on Tuesday though I am sure that will change."

Lew waited while Osborne finished pulling on the gloves. "Ready?" she asked, standing alongside Osborne. "Don't be surprised if this is nasty."

"We'll deal with it."

Gingerly, they pulled the sheets and blankets apart. The first layers exposed nothing. As they reached the lowest clump of sheets, Lew lifted the top sheet from the bed and they stared at a wet, viscous pool: small but potent.

"At least it's nothing dead ... or worse," said Osborne.

"No. But why leave such a calling card?" asked Lew. "I mean— this is something I can work with—*right now.*"

She leaned back against one of the dressers and pulled out her cell phone. "Bruce Peters," she said, using the voice activation feature. She hit the speaker button so Osborne could hear the conversation.

"Hey, Bruce, Lewellyn Ferris here," said Lew at the sound of a cheery male voice. "Sorry to call you at home on a weekend but I have a serious situation up here."

Osborne crossed his arms settled himself against the wall to listen. He checked his watch and saw it was after five. Suddenly the prospect of not having to touch anything in the bedroom or den was a welcome one.

"Chief! That's okay. Good to hear from you," said Bruce. "Hold on. Let me turn down the television—got the Packers on."

"Sure." She winked at Osborne as she waited. Bruce was her buddy—he'd come through.

Bruce Peters was in his early thirties, recently engaged and possessed of such a buoyant personality that Osborne wondered how he came to be so interested in forensic science: too often the study of bad things people do to one another. But then who knows how one finds their calling in life? How had Osborne come to love dentistry? Or fishing, for that matter?

It was fly fishing that Lew counted on to lure Bruce north. Months earlier, and not long after he had been hired by the Wausau Crime Lab, Bruce was assigned to help the Loon Lake police with a murder investigation. On arriving in Lew's office, he had noticed two artworks on the wall behind her desk.

"Like those, Bruce?" Lew had asked. "I just bought them at the Trout Unlimited Banquet—the ones on the right are Ausable Wulff trout flies tied by Francis Betters, a very famous fly fisherman and fly tyer. The other holds two of his Haystack trout flies—unsinkable but I would never fish with those. Too beautiful."

After studying the framed trout flies up close, Bruce had said, "you know, I've always wanted to learn how to fly fish but I've never met anyone who could teach me ..."

"You have now," said Lew.

That plus his sunny manner and his impeccable forensic skills prompted Lew to take him under her wing. Evenings after a day's work, she would drive him down to the Prairie River where she initiated him into the mechanics of casting, the challenge of "matching the hatch" by choosing the trout fly most likely to seduce a brook trout—and the sheer magic of an evening spent in whispering waters.

So it was that Bruce Peters had never turned down a request from Chief Lewellyn Ferris. She did not ask often but when thwarted by his superiors on critical cases, she knew whom to call.

After giving Bruce a quick overview of the computer issues at the college and the subsequent break-in at the home of the college president, she said, "this is not student vandalism. Someone with a sick agenda rampaged through here. The home office has been damaged and the president's personal computer completely destroyed.

"Bruce, I've seen vandalism by kids and vandalism by ex-wives and I would say this goes beyond either of those. The destruction, the anger, the force used to wreak this havoc—this is the product of a disturbed individual. But he did leave a calling card, which is why I hope you can help us out.

"In the bedroom, after tearing things up—our visitor left a puddle of semen in the couple's bed—"

"Great," said Bruce, "and not very smart. We may dealing with an idiot here."

"Now, Bruce, just so you know, I talked to your boss yesterday and asked for assistance on our investigation at the college and was turned down. But that's when we thought we had a student hacker. He told me that was a matter for the Feds. I tried them but they blew me off, too, but that's worked out okay. The college is paying for two consultants, experts in the fields of computer-assisted investigative reporting and digital forensics."

"Wow, I'd like to know what they know," said Bruce.

"But I need help with the results of this break-in. The nature of the vandalism makes me concerned for the personal safety of Patience Schumacher, the Wheedon College president."

Not her husband, noted Osborne. Interesting.

"Chief, I'll be there first thing in the morning," said Bruce. "Is the entire house a disaster?"

"No, just those two rooms. I've checked."

"Good. Then here's what I need you to do. Close down all access and don't allow anyone to move or touch a thing. I may be able to get some prints. Let the semen stains air dry. If all goes well, I'll get a DNA report on that ASAP. The good news is the state gave us the money to update our equipment and technology so it shouldn't take long. And I have a few favors I can call in so we can have the DNA results run through the state and national databases pronto.

"One more thing," said Bruce. "How difficult would it be for you to get DNA samples from any other males that have access to that home?"

"Would a toothbrush work? The husband is out of town right now—but he left an electric toothbrush behind. Would the brush section off that work?"

"Toothbrush is fine. Meet you at your office at eight tomorrow morning?"

"I'll be there."

"Oh, Chief, one small favor to ask …"

"Of course, Bruce. Shoot." Lew grinned at Osborne. She knew this was coming.

"Those Dead Deceivers you showed me last fall? Got any extras I might have? Hope to go north with one of my buddies this spring—fish steelhead."

"Tied some this winter, kiddo. Half a dozen are yours so long as you promise not to lose them on alder branches."

"O-o-h," said Bruce with a wince in his voice, "I'll do my best."

"Bruce," said Lew, her voice serious, "I can't thank you enough—"

"Chief, you'll pay," said Bruce, chortling as he hung up.

Just as Lew tucked her cell phone back into its holster on her hip, Patience entered the bedroom. Her shoulders were slumped and her face tear-stained. "I tried Charles but his phone must be off. I left a message."

"I don't want you staying here tonight," said Lew. "Let's get you a room at the Loon Lake Motel. I have a forensic expert from the Wausau Crime Lab who will be working here in tomorrow morning. It's critical that no one disturbs anything in the den or your bedroom until he is finished. Do you have extra clothing in another room, I hope?"

"Yes, I keep my work clothes in the guest room closet. That won't be a problem. I do think I'll sleep better at the motel."

"One more thing," said Lew. "We'll be doing some DNA testing on the bedclothes that may help us identify who broke in. But I do need one of your husband's used toothbrushes. Just a formality to rule him out—"

"What? You can't be serious. *Charles* is a suspect?"

"Everyone who may have had access to your home is a suspect," said Lew. "Simply a formality that allows us to rule him out. That's all."

But Patience was in tears again.

As they were walking to their cars, Osborne said, "Lew, Ray and I had an encounter today that I need to talk to you about."

Lew paused, her hand on the door of her cruiser. "Please tell me we have a lead on the Beltner murder."

"I wouldn't go that far, but we spent time with old Walter Frisch. He's living in an old shack out near the swamp behind the Merriman Trail. He found a snowshoe in the road by his place that we think is one of Kathy Beltner's."

"He found it in the road?" asked Lew, leaning back against the cruiser, her arms crossed and her eyes intent on Osborne's. "That's curious. As if it fell off a vehicle, maybe?"

"So we went on down the road and back in to this place I knew as a kid—the old Russian camp. Do you know the place?"

"Never heard of it. Is it like a holdover from the logging days? One of those strange old places you find in the middle of nowhere?"

"Exactly. Only a very surly fellow is squatting in there. No fire number. No mailbox. From the looks of it, he's been doing a lot of work on the place. But when Ray and I tried to talk to the joker, he ran us off the place. Insisted his property was posted, which it was not." Osborne felt his anger rising again just thinking about the guy.

"Ray is going to report him to the DNR or the Forestry Service, whichever one has jurisdiction over that land. I think we should have a search warrant to check the place out, Lew. Where he's living isn't far from where the old man found the one snowshoe."

"Did you ask him about it?"

"The creep? We tried. Like I said, he literally ran us off the place."

Lew lowered her head in thought. "It'll take a little doing with the judge, Doc. Search warrants aren't easy to come by these days. Living near a crime scene isn't 'probable cause,' I'm afraid. Let me work on it but tomorrow is the earliest I can make the call."

"I realize that. This may be a long shot but Ray and I both think we should be able to check it out."

CHAPTER 22

O sborne opened the back door to let Mike out one last time. As he waited for the dog, he checked the barometer on the mudroom wall. The barometric pressure had plummeted, signaling the approach of new snow. Just then the phone in the kitchen rang and Osborne left the inside door open as he went to answer it.

"Doc," said Lew in a worried voice, "sorry to call so late but have you any idea where Ray and Suzanne might be? It's after eleven and I know she was planning to drive home early in the morning."

"Hold on," said Osborne, "I just let the dog out. I'll step outside and see if they might be over at his place because I saw lights when I drove in."

He set the phone down and stepped out into the backyard. Winter stripped the leaves from the oaks and maples that buffered his property, making it easy to see the warm glow from the interior of his neighbor's house trailer.

Osborne picked up the phone, "Yep, from the looks of it someone's home. Want me to walk over and see what's up?"

"Would you please? I've tried both their cell phones with no luck. But, Doc, be careful. I don't want to embarrass either of them if—"

"Lewellyn, I am the father of two daughters who have put

me in this position more than once. I can handle it. Call you back in a few minutes."

"Thank you, sweetie."

Osborne hung up with a big grin on his face. He loved it when she called him names.

The night air was invigorating even though he was ready for a good night's sleep. Looking down the long drive, he was surprised to see lights out on the ice. Oh, come on. Did Ray have Suzanne out ice fishing this late? The poor girl. Osborne shook his head. Honest to Pete—what is the guy thinking?

Hurrying past the trailer home, he aimed his flashlight towards the lights on the lake. A monster bluegill was staring straight at him—bulbous eyes glinting in the moonlight, its jaws wide open to showcase two human beings sitting side by side on folding canvas chairs, their happy faces ruddy in the glow from lanterns set in the snow around the fish.

"Hey, Doc," Ray stood up, "whaddya think?"

"What on earth?" Osborne looked the fish up and down. It was a round ball about five feet in diameter and painted a dark greenish-blue with darker vertical stripes and a bright orange belly. The back of the gill facing him sported a large black dot.

"I'm entering the ice shanty contest," said Ray. "Check out the inside. Suzanne helped me make it and we finished just a few minutes ago. Cool, huh?"

"Amazing," said Osborne. He bent to peer inside. The interior was surprisingly spacious and would certainly hold at least two fishermen seated. A small propane heater sat on a circle of plywood and a lantern hanging off a hook made it feel cozy.

"How did you do this so fast?" asked Osborne.

"Pretty simple, really," offered Suzanne. "Ray had one of those pop-up portable tents so all we had to do was rig some wire fencing to give it some shape and cover it all with canvas sheeting.

I painted the canvas," said Suzanne with pride. "Nice job, don't you think?"

"She painted," said Ray, "I stapled."

"And managed to avoid stapling himself," said Suzanne with a laugh. "But I have had to listen to a lot of bad jokes.

"Sit down, Doc, and have a soda with us," said Ray.

"Thanks but I'm here because it's after eleven and someone's mother is worried," said Osborne. "Let me call your mom so she knows Ray hasn't gotten you into big trouble."

"Are you kidding? It's that late?" said Suzanne. "I had no idea. Tell her I'm on my way."

"In a minute," said Ray, pulling her back down in the chair by the sleeve of her jacket. "Let us … bask for another … two minutes … in the beauty of our creation. Then … you can leave."

"All right, twist my arm," said Suzanne, slapping her arms with her mitts to keep warm.

"Tell Doc what you're going to do."

"Oh, come on, I'm not sure about it yet," she said, hedging. "Ray's trying to talk me into a major life change, Doc."

"If … I win the contest."

"Right. If he wins the ice shanty contest, then I am supposed to sell my firm and go back to school."

"That *is* a major life change," said Osborne. "How did you two come up with that idea?"

"It's me, really," said Suzanne. "I was having such a good time doing this today that I told him how much I've always loved working making art—design, painting, drawing. I'm good at it, I know.

"But when I was getting out of high school and knew I wanted to be able to make money so I wouldn't have to dance at places like Thunder Bay—it was my guidance counselor who recommended accounting. He said people always need accountants. And he was right but after twelve years I know it's not how I want to spend my entire life."

"So ... I told her," said Ray, raising the index finger he always raised when he was convinced he had a brilliant idea, "that ... given all the change in her life because of the divorce—why not apply to a good grad school and get that Master of Fine Arts? Make change work for you. Right, Suzanne?"

She shrugged. "I'm thinking about it. I've always dreamed of going to Cranbrook Academy of Art over in Michigan. But I doubt I can get in."

"Hey, if I win the contest—you'll have that for your portfolio."

"Yeah, well ... we'll see." Suzanne got to her feet. "I gotta get going. You call me if you win, okay?"

"One more joke," said Ray, "then you can go."

Suzanne sat down again. "This is the last one and I mean it." But she smiled and Osborne could see she was reluctant to leave.

"This friend of Doc's took his wife to a restaurant—"

"Leave me out of this," said Osborne, raising a hand in resistance. He glanced at Suzanne, "I am not responsible for any of this." She laughed.

Ray ignored him, saying, "But the husband ordered first. Said he wanted the strip steak, medium rare. The waiter asked him if he was sure: 'Aren't you worried about the mad cow?' he said. 'Nah,' said Doc's friend, 'she can order for herself.'"

"See what I mean?" said Suzanne, getting to her feet as she punched Ray in the shoulder. "Really bad jokes. Okay, guys, I am out of here."

"I'll walk you up to your car," said Osborne. "Ray, you coming?"

"Okay if I stay here?" asked Ray, looking up at the cloud cover overhead. "I have a couple tip-ups I'd like to keep an eye on for awhile. With that snow coming, I think I got some hungry crappies lurking under the ice, doncha know. Suzanne, I'll see you when I see you."

Suzanne leaned down to give him a peck on the cheek. "You be sure to call me, win or lose."

"Deal."

As they reached the driveway and Suzanne's car, Osborne said, "Ray seems in very good spirits. What do you think? Your mother and I were worried that he had started drinking again."

"He seems okay now," said Suzanne. "This was a fun day for both of us. You know, Ray is a real sweetheart. But a friend, that's all." She smiled as she put the key in the ignition. "A good friend period, Dr. Osborne. I am not stupid."

CHAPTER 23

"At least we don't have to worry about the hard drive in that computer," said Beth as she and Bruce Peters picked their way through the jumble of debris, which was all that was left of the Schumacher's den. Stepping carefully so as not to dislodge anything, Doc and Lew followed behind.

It was Monday morning and Beth had been working in her office when Lew called to see if there had been any new developments in the spam investigation. On hearing that things were quiet at the moment, Lew told her of the break-in at Dr. Schumacher's.

"I would like to stop by your office and introduce you to Bruce Peters from the Wausau Crime Lab," said Lew. "He may need your help with the computer situation. Do you have the time to follow us out to Dr. Schumacher's place?"

To everyone's relief, she did. After a quick introduction to Bruce and a discussion of the need for a computer specialist to be involved, Beth had not hesitated to follow them out to Patience's home.

"What do you mean no need to worry about the hard drive?" asked Lew, astonishment on her face as she closed the door to the den door behind her. "I just told Bruce on the drive out here that we suspect the data thief who has been illegally harvesting emails from the college network may have destroyed the laptop in order to cover his tracks.

"I also told him that the illegal network access must have originated from Patience Schumacher's laptop since our thief had to have her user name and password to get into the network. Am I wrong about that?"

"Oh, you are quite right, Chief Ferris," said Beth, her voice matter of fact and unhurried. "But during the telephone conference call late yesterday afternoon with Julie, Dani and I were warned that Dr. Schumacher's laptop could hold valuable data, so we decided it would be wise to put it in a safe place as soon as possible.

"Right after our meeting, I called Dr. Schumacher and arranged for Dani to drop off a replacement computer. Her laptop is in a locked closet at the college."

"Excuse me," said Lew, checking her cellphone, "I have a call from the switchboard. Doc, would you take over please?" She walked into the next room.

"Beth, when exactly was it that you dropped off the new computer?" asked Osborne.

"Maybe three o'clock—right around then."

"So, Bruce," said Osborne, "we know Dr. Schumacher went out for an early dinner with friends, which is when we think the break-in occurred." Bruce jotted the timeframe down in his notebook.

"Okay," said Bruce, "got it. And then?"

"Since then, Dani —"

"Excuse me," said Bruce, "but who is Dani?"

"I'm sorry," said Beth, "I should have explained this earlier. Dani is a student of mine at the college, and a very good little computer tech who knows our system well. She and I have emailed Julie data footprints from the laptop as well copies of the spam messages, which Julie has forwarded to her team of techs.

"Perhaps Chief Ferris has mentioned already that Julie's crew has been working on similar email fraud investigations. When they saw our data, they immediately picked up on a pattern that confirmed something very, very interesting: our Wheedon College interloper has set up hosting in China with access to as many as twenty-five servers."

"Whew, that's amazing," said Bruce. "That was fast."

"Well, Dani was good enough to spend most of Sunday emailing all the information that we've collected so far." Beth turned to Lew, "I am not worrying over the hours she works. Does that seem okay to you, Chief Ferris?"

"Beth, whatever works," said Lew. "If there is a problem with payment, I'll negotiate that with the college. I know the family responsibilities you have so Dani's involvement is critical.

"Beth heads up the computer technology department at the college but she also has four children, a husband and the funeral arrangments for a close friend of hers who was murdered last week," Lew explained to Bruce. "Beth, whatever works for you, please.

"What I cannot stress enough is this: the minute either you or Dani see any sign of the spammer on the college computer network—and if that means they may be on the campus—you must alert me ASAP. Surveillance and apprehension is my duty. I cannot allow either of you to be placed in harm's way. Is that understood?"

"Yes. And I have made that clear to Dani, Chief Ferris," said Beth.

"Good," said Lew. "Sorry to have interrupted, please go on filling us in on the details."

"Sure," said Beth with a nod. "Julie explained to us that her tech team knew right away what to look for because it is happening everywhere. Early this morning, I had an email from Julie saying they were able to determine that whoever is doing this

has harvested around over a hundred thousand student email addresses from the tech college network across the country—and is
currently running thirty or more spam campaigns using at least
that many domain names. Did I mention that Julie told us they
make money selling the addresses to other spammers? Possibly
as much as a million bucks in this case. That's in addition to the
money they make off the fake offers."

"Wow," said Bruce, "this is hard to believe."

"Currently, they've been seducing the students with supposed
discounts on smartphones," said Beth. "First thing this morning
I made sure that all the colleges affected will have sent
out warnings, but that may be a little too late for several thousand
kids. Our worry now is that the spammers may use the students'
credit card information to commit identity theft."

"I have a question," said Bruce. "Who's this Julie person?"

"Julie's an expert on digital forensics," said Lew. "She's
a colleague of Gina Palmer's, a friend of Doc's and mine—
a professor of journalism who has a cabin up here. She's helped
our department out in the past with database-driven investigations. Julie has a broader reach when it comes to this type
of investigation.

"Currently, she is supervising a team of computer engineers
contracted by several major corporations that have experienced
fraud involving spam and identity theft. Under the umbrella
of 'digital forensics' they are designing software that can track
illegal use of computers internationally. Pretty impressive and,
I assure you, new to me. Does that answer your question?"

Bruce nodded, rapt. "Please, keep talking—you've got
my attention. I'm thinking of getting into computer forensics
myself. This is fascinating, and it's all happening at a small college
in Loon Lake?"

As they spoke, Osborne picked his way through the debris.
In one corner, a sketchbook had been torn into tiny strips. Only

the cover remained in one piece; on it, Charles had written his name and phone number and the words "in case this is lost, please return to." Whoa, thought Osborne, looks like Charles' name alone was enough to set off the intruder.

"Bruce," said Lew, "the reality is simple: the crime may be occurring via the Internet but the perpetrator is launching it from a computer located somewhere under our noses here on the Wheedon College campus. I have to apprehend that person or people— and soon." Lew shook her head, "what frustrates me is the fact this is a federal crime and I'm getting no support from the FBI."

Beth nodded in agreement. "I'm with you, Chief. And besides the fraud, the spammer has installed viruses that have infected the hard drives on a number of our computers. It's costing us a lot of money.

"But I'll tell you one thing: after this experience, I'm going to recommend we develop a curriculum on computer forensics."

"That will put Wheedon College on the map," said Bruce.

"You better believe it," said Lew, thinking as she spoke how lucky it was that they had had Gina Palmer to make the connection to the digital forensic experts. Better yet—Wheedon College was equally fortunate to have someone like Beth on staff.

"What if you didn't have advice from this woman Julie?" asked Bruce. "What then?"

"Chief Ferris and I talked about this," said Beth with a nod towards Lew, "We—meaning the college—would be at the mercy of the spammer until whoever it is decided they had mined enough money and information from the students and moved on to a new target."

"How much money are we talking about?" asked Bruce.

"Yes," asked Osborne, "what is the estimate at this point?"

"Correct me if I'm wrong, Beth," said Lew, "but Julie advised us it could run up to a million dollars or more. These poor college kids have given up their credit cards and bank information thinking all these offers are coming from the school. Now that the spam is making its way through this network to all the other tech colleges," Lew raised her hands in a gesture of helplessness, "who knows how much damage will be done."

"That much?" Osborne was stunned. "Unbelievable the reach the spammers have once they're inside an entire network. All that from a single, solitary computer?"

"Right," said Beth. "We've been able to prove that the initial spam was sent under Dr. Schumacher's name and the data footprint confirms it originated from her laptop. We have to assume that whoever is at the heart of this operation must have—or had—access to this house. Dr. Schumacher has a desktop computer in her office at the college, but the home office laptop was the source of the initial messages."

"Her husband maybe?" asked Bruce, his eyebrows raised. "Or kids? Does she have teenagers?"

"No children. And, yeah, the husband is a definite suspect, which is why I made sure that Dr. Schumacher would not be here this morning. The woman is overwrought as it is so until I have enough evidence to consider the husband 'a person of interest' ..." Lew hesitated as she gazed around the room.

"Given what Beth just told us about substituting a computer—one with different settings and no access to the college network—for the original laptop makes it easy to explain what we see here: our spammer was so upset to find the original laptop gone that he went berserk. Threw a homicidal temper tantrum Thank goodness Patience was not home or she may have been assaulted."

"Wow," said Bruce, repeating himself and shaking his head. "I guess it's not surprising if you estimate that the access has been worth over a million bucks—but he has to realize you're on to him and it's only a matter of time. But, hey, how does this person access the money?"

"It's quite easy," said Beth. "Payments from credit card orders and fees from other spammers are made through a legitimate service like PayPal and that money is forwarded to an account in a bank somewhere. It can be traced but by the time that happens—"

"The account has been emptied," said Lew.

"Or moved off-shore," volunteered Osborne.

"Hmm," Bruce chewed on a knuckle. "Why the hell would he leave semen on the bed? If your person of interest is the expert he appears to be then my guess is he's committed previous crimes, and if he's been caught in the past I may well get a DNA match off our criminal databases."

"Maybe he wants to be caught?" said Lew, turning to face the group. "Maybe this is a sick person? Maybe he's someone who has *easy* access to the house. Patience said her husband is out of town at a conference but we have no proof of that. Yet."

"How many people have had access to these two rooms?" asked Bruce.

"Six of us," said Lew. "Myself and Doc, Patience and her husband Charles, of course.

"Plus Dani and myself," said Beth. "Dani brought in the new laptop but both of us may have touched the desk, the router, the modem, the cords ..."

"Then I would like to fingerprint everyone," said Bruce. "Makes it easier to isolate any rogue prints that might reinforce any DNA match I may get."

"Sounds good to me," said Lew.

"Something else I'd like to mention," said Beth. "When I was working with Dani at the college yesterday, our vice president of operations pulled me aside to ask about the spamming. When I told him that Dr. Schumacher had nothing to do with the spam that appeared to originate from her, he was quite relieved and said he would notify the board of trustees ASAP.

"Chief, I know you've said that Dr. Schumacher is certain she is being stalked here and at the college but I can't imagine anyone related to the college administration being involved.

"I mean, for heaven's sake, our annual budget depends on funding generated by the Schumacher family trust and Dr. Schumacher has complete control over that. But we know she is often less confident than she appears. She has been prone to feeling persecuted before. That worries those of us who work with her."

"Paranoid, in other words?" asked Bruce.

"Could be," said Lew. "Her husband, Charles, has shared with us that at one time she thought that he was stealing from her."

Bruce's eyebrows rose. "Not the case, I take it?"

"Not according to him," said Lew.

"We've got an unusual situation here," said Osborne. "Patience and her husband met just last year when he was hired by the general contractor remodeling this house to do interior detail work. You know, paint walls, put up molding—that sort of thing. She fell in love with the guy and they got married. Bang, just like that. Now she bankrolls him to do fine art."

"So we have a very wealthy woman and a guy with no money," said Bruce.

"Yep," said Lew. "And we have no history on the guy. He's not from the area. No family, no other friends that we're aware of. He's the elephant in the room."

"Well, well," said Bruce. "To start with—what I would like to do is take the damaged laptop with me. Chances are that whoever left his calling card on the bed wasn't too concerned with leaving a trail of any kind. If he grabbed the laptop and threw it, I could get some good prints. I'll work both rooms but the laptop exterior could be a mother lode."

"Beth, anything more before we meet with Patience and, hopefully, Charles?" asked Lew. "After hearing from Patience,

Charles decided to leave the art seminar early. He's due home this morning, Bruce. Anytime now."

"Just to say that Dani is doing great," said Beth. "She has been able to pinpoint three different computers where our data thief has plugged into Ethernet connections on campus—two classrooms and one administrative office. The data footprint indicates he operates late in the evenings. What's curious is he or she or they—we don't know for sure yet if we're dealing with one or more people—does not appear to use the college wi-fi."

A knock at the door of the den prompted Lew to raise a finger to her lips. She said in a low voice, "Let's keep everything we said here confidential for the moment."

"This is unbelievable," said Charles as he walked from the den to the bedroom. "Dearest," he put an arm across Patience's broad shoulders, "I wish you had told me how severe the damage was. I would have driven home sooner."

Patience turned sad eyes on him. "What good would that have done? We couldn't stay here last night and at least you were able to finish your class."

Her husband squeezed her arm, "You are always thinking of others."

And I am thinking of *you*, thought Osborne. He and Lew had already decided to check on Charles' alleged art seminar. Was he really in Milwaukee? Did he have someone who could verify that?

"Speaking of others," said Lew, "Charles, do you have any idea who might have done this? We're working on the premise that this is likely related to the computer fraud but anything else come to mind? Any person you are aware of who might be holding a grudge against you? Or your wife?"

Charles shook his head.

"Patience?" said Lew, "I know I've asked you this before—

any new ideas?"

"No," said Patience. "I stopped by my office this morning though and ran into Dani. She said she was working on the computer network last night and was able to monitor spam coming in so she went down to check—"

"What time last night?" said Beth, interrupting. "Chief Ferris, twice now I have told that young woman that she is not to approach anyone who may be using the network unless I'm there, too. If she sees something, she's to alert both myself and you. Oh, this is upsetting."

"And very risky," said Lew. "From now on, when either of you is on campus at a time when you expect to see activity in the system—I want to be there, too. Understood?"

"Absolutely," said Beth. "I'm no action hero. I know Dani needs the money and wants to put in as many hours as she can but I have made it very clear: we are looking for an individual who is committing a crime and could be dangerous. But, you know? Loon Lake is such a nice little town, I can see from the expression on her face she doesn't take me seriously. Look, I'll hammer this into her before I leave today."

"Going back to what Dani told me," said Patience, "it was after nine that she saw an Ethernet connection in use down in the culinary arts classroom but when she got there the room was empty, lights off. Think she made a mistake?"

"Doesn't matter. That is exactly what I do not want her— or Beth—doing," said Lew, angry. "They see something—they call me. I keep my cell on 24/7. Make sure she knows that will you, Beth?"

Beth nodded. Exhaustion crept across her face and Osborne speculated that in spite of her recent tragedy, the family and the funeral plans for her murdered friend, she was still staying close to the investigation. Likely not getting much sleep, but a trouper.

He caught Lew's eye and her expression was grim. He would be sleeping alone until this was resolved. No way would Lew allow those young women to be working alone on campus during the hours the spam was entering the system.

CHAPTER 24

Two hours later, Bruce Peters was on Highway 51 heading south to the Wausau Crime Lab with evidence packages containing the stained bedclothes and the remains of the laptop computer. He had spent most of his time gathering fingerprints from both rooms and from all five individuals. Charles had not hesitated to be printed. Nor had he balked when Bruce asked for a DNA sample.

After helping Bruce load his van, Doc invited Lew and Beth to join him for a quick lunch at the Loon Lake Pub.

"I am beginning to wonder if Charles Mason is bipolar or something," said Lew over her tuna salad, and giving a quick glance around to be sure she wasn't speaking too loud. But the restaurant was packed and the noise level high enough to hide anything short of a shriek.

"I find him hard to read. One minute he's so low-key it's like he's on meds. But when he talks with his voice so high and tight, it's as if he's really tense." She decided not to mention the inappropriate phone call in front of Beth.

"He never makes eye contact," said Doc, unrolling the paper napkin taped around a knife and fork. "Not a good sign in my opinion but I'm no psychiatrist."

"You're right!" said Lew, pointing her fork. "I *knew* there was something. That's a control issue, I think. I'll have to look it up. Beth, what do you think? He's fairly attractive, right?"

Osborne answered before Beth could finish chewing a cracker she had buttered. "Attractive, Chief? With that grey skin and those skinny legs? You must kidding—he doesn't look healthy."

"I didn't ask you, Doc," said Lew with a twinkle in her eye. "Beth?"

"Certainly better-looking than Dr. Schumacher," said Beth, "but he's got one of those bland faces you have a hard time remembering. I wouldn't call him handsome, Chief Ferris, but something about him does catch your eye. Speaking of Dr. Schumacher—she seems on the verge of tears all the time She isn't always like that. I'm surprised. Especially now that we can reassure her that she did nothing to cause the breaching of the computer system.

"She's got an excuse these days," said Lew with a sigh. "Dr. Patience Schumacher does not have much under control. How long have you worked at the college, Beth?"

"Almost three years. I guess ... if you want my opinion, I think she tries hard, too hard, to live up to what she imagines her father would do. She makes little asides that—again this is my opinion—imply she's always second-guessing her decisions. She isn't happy in her own skin if you know what I mean."

As Beth spoke, Osborne was struck by her level-headedness, the quiet authority with which she expressed herself. Like Lew. Is that what is meant by being 'happy in your own skin?'"

Lew was quiet, finishing the lemon chicken soup that she had ordered. The three of them ate industriously, cleaning their plates of the home-cooked food the Pub was known for. Finally, Lew spoke, "Something about that couple reminds me of a case we studied when I was in law enforcement classes.

"A high school teacher was accused of having sexual relations with one of his female students, a junior just fifteen years old, and it turned out that she was one of many girls he had victimized over his career. When he was finally exposed as a serial predator of young women, he gave an interview to a group of psychologists in which he said that the moment a new class of students walked into his classroom, he knew which girls were emotionally vulnerable. Knew it instantly.

"I feel like Patience Schumacher has always been one of those emotionally weak women."

"A natural victim?" asked Osborne. "That's a sad thought."

"An easy mark," said Lew. Beth threw her a concerned look as though she wasn't sure exactly what Lew meant.

"She certainly didn't marry a man like her father," said Osborne. "That guy was as tall as Charles but strong, intimidating. Hearty, loud—you sure knew when he was in the room. I have a hunch he would not be happy with his daughter's choice of a husband."

"Who happens to be next on my list," said Lew. "I would like to know just where Charles Mason has been these last forty-eight hours. As soon as I'm back in the office, I'm calling the university—see if he really was attending a seminar. She handed her plate and soup bowl to the waitress and said, "I imagine I'll be in voice mail hell trying to find the right people who would know."

"Let me try," said Beth, rummaging in her purse before pulling out an iPhone. I got this for my birthday and it is so cool. If you don't mind, let's allow technology to save you some time." With that, Beth flashed her first smile of the day. "Watch," she said, holding the phone so Lew could see her fingers work. "It is so amazing." And she was right. Within seconds, the iPhone had located the number for the university art department. Beth put the call through and handed the phone to Lew.

"Hello," said Lew when a young male voice answered. She introduced herself and explained that she was interested in confirming that a certain individual had attended a recent two-day seminar held on the campus. Beth and Osborne listened as she spoke.

"I believe you are calling about the encaustic and emulsion seminar," said the man. "I'm one of the grad students who organized it. I am afraid I can't answer your question as we had over a thousand people attend. They did not have to register beforehand but paid at the door. It's one of our 'Learning in Retirement' programs that we offer to the general public every month."

"Do the people attending stay on campus?" asked Lew.

"I would have no way of knowing that," said the man. "The majority of the attendees are local and go home after the various workshops. Sorry I can't be of more help."

"I don't suppose you would have any photos or video of the people attending the seminar?" Lew grimaced as she asked the question knowing it was a long shot.

"No, sorry—but wait, there is one thing that may help you. Everyone had an opportunity to buy materials in order to participate in the workshops. Why don't you check to see if your person bought any of those?"

"Thank you," said Lew. "Well." She looked around the table and pushed her plate away. "Maybe it's a start. Maybe not. This is frustrating. Plus I've already run a background check through our police records and found nothing under the name of Charles Mason."

Beth was taking a final sip of her coffee as Lew spoke. "What about public records? Have you researched those? I teach a class on search engines and it's amazing what is available online. Court reports, divorce agreements, tax liens. People do not realize how much information they think is confidential—is not.

I have time this afternoon to do a public record search if that's okay with you?"

"That would be helpful, Beth. It might be wise for me to bring you on board as a subject matter expert—a short-term deputy specific to this case—if that's not a problem for the college. Let's head over to my office and I'll have you complete the paperwork. Sure you have time?"

"I do today. The funeral Mass and wake for Kathy Beltner is not until Friday and all the arrangements have been made. We're waiting for her son to return—he was in Germany. Junior year abroad. I'll just need Charles Mason's full name. Does he have a middle initial?"

"F. For Franklin," said Lew. "I'm pretty sure. I'll check when I get back to my desk but they put their full names on a form I had them fill out after our first meeting."

"The middle initial will certainly help. If we're going to meet over at the police department, would it be too much trouble to include Dani? I'll get the records search started but I may have to hand it over to her ... "

"In that case, I should have her deputized the same as yourself. Covers the legality of any search results. Do you think she's available to meet in half an hour?"

"I'll give her a call," said Beth as she reached again for her iPhone. After a brief conversation, Beth looked back to Lew. "She sounds excited about being deputized," said Beth with a soft grin.

But then a look of concern crossed Beth's face. "Wait," she said, "maybe this isn't such a good idea. I work for Dr. Schumacher and now I'm running a background check on her husband? That could get me fired and Dani expelled. Chief Ferris, can you find someone else to do it?"

"I take full responsibility," said Lew. "It's my business and only my business who I employ to run a records search.

Dr. Schumacher does not have to know—that is confidential information."

"Good," said Beth, "I feel better knowing that. And, frankly, I think we're doing it to protect Dr. Schumacher, right?"

"Yes. We may find absolutely nothing out of the ordinary about Charles and that helps the college investigation, too. Are you comfortable with this, Beth? We'll have to be sure that Dani knows to keep this confidential as well."

"I'll take care of that," said Beth. "Oh, and by the way," she said, holding her iPhone up so Lew and Osborne could see the screen, "I took a picture of the gentleman in question when he wasn't watching. Got one of Bruce Peters, too. And you two. Thought the photos might be nice to have in case there are images of anyone named Charles F. Mason on the Internet. Any problem with that, Chief?"

"Fine with me," said Lew, getting to her feet. "If you two don't mind, it's time to head back." Lew glanced at Beth, "Sorry to rush off but I need to check on my two officers who have been holding down the fort for me. Today is the official opening of the fishing tournament. Keeping my fingers crossed that we have no crowd problems.

"Doc, I have to call Rob Beltner back sometime today. He sent me an email this morning asking if we had any leads on his wife's death. I sure hope something breaks soon," said Lew, a defeated look on her face. She pulled her parka on.

"I am certainly not law enforcement," said Beth, her voice cracking as she reached for her jacket, "but ... you know ... if I can do anything to help." Tears welled in her eyes and she reached into her pocket for a Kleenex. Lew gave her shoulders a sympathetic squeeze. Osborne looked away. Sadness is catching.

Minutes later, as Osborne followed Lew's cruiser back to the department in his own car, his cell phone rang.

"Doc," said Lew, "I just walked in and was told that an old guy stopped by early this morning with a note for Ray. Looks to be from his friend, Walter Frisch, who wants him to stop by his place. Said he found what Ray has been looking for."

"Really? Did he say anything else?" asked Osborne.

A moment's silence, than Lew said, "If I can read his scrawl, I'll give you the exact message, which is and I quote: "C'mon out— found what you're looking for —in the garage.'"

"I'll get Ray and we'll drive out there right away. If we're lucky, he found the other snowshoe."

Osborne drove through town and up the north side to Squirrel Lake where the fishing tournament was underway. He paused at the top of a hill to look down at the huge tents that had been set up along the shoreline to house the vendors and the events. Trucks bearing the names of the participating teams filled the parking lot near the tents.

Out on the lake, he could see the colorful teams of fishermen hovering over holes in the ice. Each team had been assigned a specific location and clusters of bystanders huddled at polite distances to watch the jigging. Looking off to his right, he saw that the ice shanties for the contest had been set up a good half mile from the fishing area so as not to disturb the hungry residents beneath the ice.

Overhead, the late afternoon sun was turning the sky a faint lavender that highlighted a scattering of flat granite clouds: a squadron of flying saucers. Gazing down on the scene before him, Osborne felt a sudden ache for summer. He was ready to trade the flat, grey-white slab stretching to the far shore for diamond-dusted ripples over azure waters under a setting August sun. But that was months away.

Putting his car into four-wheel drive, he tackled the temporary roadway that had been plowed along the shoreline towards the ice shanties. Over two dozen huts had been set up and the décor reflected their owner's passions or sense of humor. Colorful shanties heralded the Green Bay Packers and Harley-Davidson while others pretended to be mock outhouses. At least three were pricey mini-mansions sporting satellite television dishes. And then—like a visitor from another planet—was the big, fat bug-eyed bluegill with the orange belly.

"Ray?" called Osborne through the open flap that passed for an entrance.

"Yeah, Doc, what's up?" hollered Ray from inside.

"You got a message from Walter that he found what we've been looking for. We need to get out to his place. Let's go."

"Hold on. I've got to finish setting up. The contest starts at four and I want to be ready for the judges. Hey, I'm calling my shanty 'Benny the Bluegill.' Like it?"

"Do you have to be here when they come through?" Osborne checked his watch. It was only three o'clock.

"Yep. We'll drive out after that."

"If you don't mind, I'm going to go on ahead. You could be here for awhile."

Osborne did not want to wait around. Ever since Lew gave him the message, a sense of urgency had been building in his gut. It had already been hours since the old man had stopped by the station. Or maybe it was remembering the expression of defeat on Lew's face when she thought of Kathy Beltner.

"Go ahead, Doc. After you talk to Walter, give me a call. Let me know what he found."

In less than twenty minutes, Osborne had reached the logging lane that Walter used to get to his shack. He drove slowly in the fading light, the sides of his car scraped by crystalline branches of barren ghost trees. He was relieved that this trip out to Walter's was much easier than when he and Ray had parked on the other road and walked in.

It was dark by four-thirty and Osborne prayed for an early moon as he parked alongside Walter's pick-up. He opened the glove compartment to grab a flashlight then got out of the car, keeping the beam of the flashlight on the ground at his feet to avoid slipping on the icy patches dotting the walkway up to the cabin.

Twenty feet from the door, Osborne paused. He ran the beam of the flashlight across the front of the little hut. The door was ajar with no light coming from inside. Strange. He couldn't imagine the old man out walking so late in the day when it becomes difficult to see even if you have young eyes and Walter's were definitely not young.

"Walter?" He pushed the door open further and waited. No sound. "Hello, Walter—it's Doc Osborne. Ray Pradt's friend. We got your message."

Osborne ran the light around the room. The room was empty. In the shadows, he could see that the daybed had been pushed away from the wall and jutted into the room at angle. On the floor at one end of the bed was a small black area rug bunched up. No sign of the old man.

But his truck was here. He had to be somewhere. Of course, thought Osborne, I'll bet he's out back cooking on that little grill of his. Walter's hearing wasn't the best and he probably hadn't heard Osborne drive up. "Walter!" he called loudly as he walked back past the lean-to with the empty water jugs and around to the rear of the shack where Walter had his tiny Weber grill. No sign of the man.

Osborne stood, pondering. He went back to the front of the shack. Again he pushed the door open and checked the room. The angle of the daybed worried him, now that he looked more closely.

He ran the beam of the flashlight over the little rug. It shone wet under the light. Osborne leaned down to touch it: blood.

As he knelt, he spotted a figure on the floor wedged into the space behind the daybed. Walter had fallen behind the bed and likely cracked his skull on the small table alongside the bed.

Moving quickly, Osborne pulled the bed away and reached for one of the old man's arms to check for a pulse. As Walter's body rolled back with the tug, Osborne's flashlight caught the damage done to the old man's head: his face was gone. But enough of the crown of his bald head remained—proof that this was the old man who had made it to the age of ninety-two.

Osborne pushed the bed back further as if to make Walter Frisch as comfortable as possible. Now he could see that blood was seeping through the floorboards of the old shack. A sudden chill passed across his shoulders—was the killer still here?

Hustling to his feet, Osborne ran for his car, jumped in and locked all the doors. Breathing heavily he waited, watching. But there was no one close. Hands shaking, he called Lew.

Leaning back relaxed in her chair, Lew listened to Beth and Dani who were sitting across from her in her office. "I will be working up until five thirty and Dani will take over at that time," said Beth. "Okay with you, Dani?"

Dani's cheery moonface nodded. "Sure. I love this search engine stuff. That's how I found out my stepdad was married twice before he married my mom. Cool stuff."

"Chief Ferris, we have a pattern of the spammer entering the system as early as eight o'clock in the evening and as late as midnight," said Beth. "Now, we are agreed—and Dani, please listen hard—that a Loon Lake officer is the only person allowed to approach a person using a campus computer. Correct?"

"Correct," said Dani, with a look that reminded Lew of a kid who promises not to lick the frosting on the cake. "I know this is serious but it has been kind of fun."

"Fun, how?" asked Lew. "Is the technology enough to lure you away from life as a cosmetician?"

Dani giggled. "Maybe. But working late like this, I've gotten to know one of the janitors." She gave a sheepish grin. "He's really nice and a funny guy. He bought me coffee during my break. Who knows," she said with a shake of her shoulders, "I might score another cup tonight. Hope so anyway."

"That's nice," said Lew, aware that any attention from a guy would make Dani happy. She had to have some reason to spend hours curling all that hair.

As Dani burbled on, Lew saw Beth check her watch. Clearly Beth was not the type to make time for girlish chat. "Yeah," said Dani, "I told him he's too old for me but I might let him take me snowmobiling ..."

"Dani—" Lew interrupted, "I'll be at the college tonight by six at the latest. If you spot any activity before then, call my cell phone. Is that clear?"

"Yes," said Dani, her giddiness in check.

"We haven't seen anything that early," said Beth.

"Ok, ladies, we're set for this evening. See you later, Dani," said Lew, walking them to the door.

After they left, Lew sat down at her desk. She smiled to herself. As stressful as the days were right now, getting to know Beth and effervescent Dani—and observing the power of technology to extend an investigation in ways that could never have happened even ten years ago—made her work so much more interesting. She would have to keep her eyes open and watch for ways the three of them might work together again. If Dani could be persuaded against a career in cosmetology.

CHAPTER 25

Within half an hour of Osborne's call, Lew arrived at Walter's place with the ambulance crew right behind her. After establishing a single entrance and exit route to keep the paramedics from disturbing any possible tracks, she was about to enter Walter's shack when Ray called to say he was half a mile away.

"We'll wait for you before we move the body," said Lew. Putting her cell phone away, she turned to Osborne. "I wonder if the victim has any family?" she asked. "I've always thought of him as the old hermit who lived out there on the lake road all alone. I never even knew his name until this happened."

"Yes, he has family—a niece and nephews, I believe," said Osborne. "The niece owns that property where you used to see Walter, though she doesn't live up here. I'll stop by a neighbor's place and see if they have any contact information."

Osborne turned as he was talking to see Ray's pick-up pull in behind his car. Ray leapt from his truck and headed straight for the shack. Lew held the door open with a gloved hand and stepped back to let him in. "Take your time," she said, "but don't touch anything, okay?"

Ray nodded and went inside. Waiting just outside the door, Osborne watched as Ray knelt to study the old man's body where it lay wedged between the daybed and the wall. Then he stood and walked outside to join Lew and Osborne, shaking his head as he said, "Damn it, I wish I had checked the front desk at the station this morning but it didn't even occur to me. If I hadn't been so busy screwing around with that goddamn stupid ice shanty this wouldn't have happened. This is my fault."

"No, Ray," said Osborne in a low, measured tone. "If we had *both* been thinking when we were first here, we would have encouraged Walter to call one or the other of us."

"He doesn't have a phone!" Ray's eyes were glassy with emotion.

"Wal-Mart has a pay phone," said Osborne. "Look, you can't blame yourself for this. The old man wasn't stupid. He knew what we were looking for and why. If he had felt any urgency, he would have asked Marlaine on the front desk to get the message to you right away. He didn't."

Ray was quiet. "You're right, I suppose, but still ..." Osborne rubbed his shoulder in sympathy.

"Tough to be accurate on time of death due to these very cold temperatures, which delay rigor," said Osborne, "and that the propane heater appears to have been turned off—but enough rigor has set in that I'm pretty sure he's been dead since before noon today."

"That bullet in his forehead," said Ray, "he was *executed*. Wait 'til I meet the joker who did that. Just wait."

"Ray, I had no idea you knew this man so well," said Lew.

"I've known him since I was a kid. We were all kind of scared of him. One day I stopped by on my bike and we got to talking. Turned out he wasn't an ogre after all. A friendly old soul he is ... was. Hell, I put him at the top of my fish list. I was planning to drop by with my catch of the day at least once a week."

And make sure he was okay, thought Osborne. Ray had a list of folks like Walter—elderly and infirm—whom he would check on and expect nothing in return. It was one reason Osborne and some of his other coffee buddies put up with the lousy jokes. When it came to good souls, Ray had one.

"The door was open when Doc got here so I'm thinking Walter must have let in someone he knew," said Lew.

"I doubt the lock on that door would keep anyone out regardless," said Ray in a grim tone, hands on his hips. "What about the garage?" he asked. "The note said he found something in the garage. Have you checked?" he asked Osborne.

"Right away," said Osborne. "I looked around while I waited for Lew to get here. All I could see was that pile of empty water jugs. Nothing unusual in the cabin either as far as I can tell. The old guy only had a few clothes and packages of cookies and stuff. Everything is stacked as neat as it was when we were here. But you should check, too."

Ray walked around to the side of the shed and stood surveying the contents. "Right, Doc. I don't see anything different."

"After they move the body, the place will be gone over very carefully," said Lew. "I'm going to have Todd handle the crime scene. Be nice to find that bullet casing. He should be out here shortly—and we'll decide if we need to include the Wausau boys on this."

"Count on me to be here looking for tracks first thing in the morning, Chief," said Ray. "We haven't had any new snow in the last few days so I might have some luck, especially if the person who did this parked elsewhere and walked in."

"Good," said Lew.

Later that evening, shortly after seven, after dropping Osborne off at her office to complete Walter's death certificate, Lew drove out to the college. Even though she had called from the crime scene to let Dani know she would be late, she was worried that some activity might have occurred with the spammer.

Just to be sure, she had admonished Dani for the umpteenth time not to pursue checking the location of any computer that might be in use. "Oh, I know," said Dani, sounding as if Chief Ferris was making a big deal over nothing.

"Dani?" said Lew on her cell phone as she drove, "I'll be there in ten minutes. Everything okay?"

"Yes indeed," said Dani. "I started to find some really, really good stuff so I called Professor Hellenbrand. She just got here and boy—oh, hold on, she wants to speak to you ..."

"Chief Ferris?" said Beth. "You will be very interested in what Dani has discovered. Things are under control at my house so I decided to drive over. We aren't finished yet either. Glad you're gonna make it."

"Be there shortly," said Lew. Both Beth and Dani sounded so excited, they must be on to something. Lew pressed harder on the accelerator.

"So sorry to be late," said Lew, entering the office where Dani and Beth sat eyes glued to a computer monitor. "We have another homicide on our hands."

"Oh no," said Beth, getting to her feet from where she had been sitting beside Dani who was working the keyboard. "No one I know I hope."

"I doubt it and I can't share the victim's name until we reach the family," said Lew, "but it may be related to the death of your friend. Same general area—out near the ski trails. Impossible to say if the same weapon was used but the victim was shot. Pretty sad, too. An old man who managed to reach the age of ninety-two only to have some jabone put a bullet through his brain."

"Sorry to hear that, Chief," said Beth, beckoning for Lew to take her place in the chair beside Dani. " But we have some good news if that would help. Good news for us at least— not so great for Dr. Schumacher, I'm afraid."

"If it has to do with our fraudster out here, I sure could use a break," said Lew.

"Our public records search on Charles F. Mason has yielded some ve-r-r-y interesting information," said Beth, her face the most animated Lew had ever seen it. "First, my search of national databases showed about four thousand Charles Masons but only three with the middle initial "F." Next I went into LexusNexus and got it narrowed to a former resident of Minneapolis. That seemed promising. That's when I turned it over to Dani. I had to get home, get the kids some dinner. Dani, tell Chief Ferris what you found."

Dani pushed her curls behind her ears and looked up at Lew as she spoke.

"So cool, Chief Ferris. I found notices of three divorce hearings and several liens against someone named Charles F. Mason. Since a lawyer's name was attached to the most recent divorce notice, I emailed that person, who happened to be online at the time, and said we might be researching the same guy. That's when I called Professor Hellenbrand for the first time.

"Yes," said Beth, "Dani called a little over an hour ago with the lawyer's email address so I emailed that photo that I took this morning. Gosh," said Beth with a sudden pained look, "I hope that was okay."

"Fine," said Lew.

Dani and Beth exchanged glances as if to relish the moment. Then Beth said in a determined tone, "He's our man. He's the same man that Dr. Schumacher married. You can see for yourself." She pointed to the computer screen where Beth's photo was displayed alongside a photo of five people in a meeting in the divorce lawyer's office. The only difference was that Charles F. Mason on that day was wearing a white shirt open at the neck under a navy blue blazer. More businessman than artist.

"Divorced three times?" asked Lew. "Over what period of time are we talking?"

"Fifteen years or so," said Beth. "Divorced twice. We aren't sure but he may still be married to Number Three."

"*And* to Patience Schumacher?" Lew rolled her eyes at the two women.

"The lawyer said he had been looking for Mr. Mason for over a year," said Dani. "But he retired last fall and turned the divorce case over to a partner in his former firm."

"Right," interjected Beth. "I called him on the phone when I got here to be sure we, you know, weren't jumping to conclusions. He's checking the status of the case tomorrow.

"He's doubtful that the divorce has gone through because the woman involved wanted a hundred thousand dollars paid back. The law office did a money search but found nothing. That's why he said he doubts Charles Mason has that kind of money and Wife Number Three wasn't going to let him off the hook until she was paid."

"Wow," said Lew, half leaning against a nearby desk. "Wow."

"The lawyer was nice enough to take the time to give me the background on Mr. Mason," said Beth. "Seems he has never made much money but always managed to land jobs at places like Target or Best Buy. He would keep each job until he met a woman who fell for him, they would marry, he would persuade her to put his name on a joint bank account and about a year into the marriage, he would empty the account and take off. A pattern."

"Did he say if these women were fellow employees or customers?"

"Both," said Beth. "One had been his manager and the other bought a home entertainment center from him, which he helped install and never left. That's what the lawyer said," said Beth with a hint of humor. Lew had a hunch that if Beth weren't in the throes of grief over the death of her close friend that she might have more of a lively, dry wit than first appeared.

"What are the liens about?" asked Lew.

"Dani," said Beth, "you found that data. What's the story on those?"

By now Dani's girlish mannerism had morphed into a sense of authority that Lew found more reassuring. "Lawsuits from the women involved," said the girl, hitting keys and leaning towards the screen as she spoke. "One wanted a car back; the other was out a chunk of her savings that he was supposed to use as a down payment on a house but never did." Dani scrolled down, looking for more. "Guess that's what I've got so far, Chief Ferris."

Lew, arms crossed and thinking back over the details, said "So basically, we have a gentleman who prefers ladies with generous bank accounts. That would include Dr. Schumacher, wouldn't it."

Beth and Dani nodded in agreement.

"There's more from the lawyer," said Beth. "I kept thinking I was keeping him from his dinner but he was really ready to talk. It's personal stuff—but do you want to hear—"

"For heaven's sake, yes," said Lew. "You know, Beth, it takes skill to get people to open up, especially lawyers. You're good." Beth blushed at the compliment.

"Apparently the ladies he wed found him quite charming and colorful. He told his first wife his hobby was raising bald eagles."

"No," said Lew, "how pretentious. And she believed him? Honestly. Keep going."

Beth looked down at her notes. "Wendy—that's Wife Number Two—was told he wanted to become a master gardener. But in the divorce documents she states that after they married, he never picked up a shovel. Wife Number Three married him thinking he was a frustrated poet ..."

"And Patience Schumacher thinks he's a painter of fine art," said Lew. "What crap! Dani," Lew shook a finger at the young woman, "you learn from this—don't ever let a guy bullshit you, okay?"

Dani giggled. "Promise."

Beth smiled, then said, "but here is the frustrating part—we have found no indication that Mr. Mason has anything but the most rudimentary experience with computers. Otherwise I would suspect him as our fraudster."

"Too bad," said Lew. "We need to confirm whether or not he is married to that another woman."

"The lawyer is having the law office send the divorce documents over by courier tomorrow. I've arranged for the package to be delivered to your office, Chief. You can expect them by late morning."

"Once they arrive, I'll get Mr. Mason in for questioning."

"That should be interesting," said Beth, slipping her notepad into her purse. "Okay, I'm heading home now. Dani is going to do a little more work on this search tonight if that's okay?"

"Fine," said Lew. "You go. I'll stay here with Dani until we call it an evening. So far no sign of the spammer, correct?"

"Nothing yet," said Dani as she waved goodnight to Beth.

Lew took the chair next to Dani. "Poor Dr. Schumacher," she said with a shake of her head. "I hate having to be the person to tell her the truth about Charles Franklin Mason."

The evening passed slowly. Not once did the cursor move that had been set up to signal the presence of spam. Around ten o'clock, Dani decided she needed a quick break for water and the bathroom.

And, thought Lew, the cute janitor, of course.

Before leaving the room, Dani said, "what you want to watch for, Chief Ferris, is this."

She showed Lew how the cursor would react if spam entered the system. "But it has always arrived by this time so I think it isn't going to happen tonight."

"How do you know that?" asked Lew. "We've only been watching for a night."

"Oh, Chief Ferris, that's not true exactly. For two weeks now, Professor Hellenbrand and I have been watching the spam coming in—and there has been a real pattern to it. That's before we knew it was originating from within the system. No, whoever it is has always sent the emails by now."

"Okay, I'll watch," said Lew.

Nothing moved. All that happened was someone entertaining Dani at the vending machines—at least Lew heard her peals of laughter before she returned to the office.

"Oh, that guy," said Dani, bouncing into the room. "He's so cute."

"Which guy are we talking about?" said Lew.

"The janitor—the one who wants to take me snowmobiling." She sat down, a grin of delight on her face. "He's got a neat beard, kinda like my dad's," she gestured towards her chin, "and these huge dark eyes. Long lashes. Cool looking guy."

"Dani," warned Lew, "I thought you said he's a lot older."

"Yeah," said Dani, raising both arms to shake her curls back behind her ears. "He is. I keep telling him that." She gave a small secret smile and Lew could see she felt very flattered. "But you know, the longer you've worked here, the more money you make."

"I assume he told you that."

"Uh huh."

Lew resisted the urge to tell her to be careful. She had delivered enough instructions tonight. At ten-thirty, they put the computer to sleep and walked to their cars in the parking lot. Parked on the walkway running alongside the maintenance garage, which was located at the far end of the parking lot, Lew saw a red snowmobile. She bet anything that was the sled Dani was hoping to ride.

Some things never change: girls like guys with cool cars ... or sleds. Lew knew. She made that mistake herself once upon a time.

CHAPTER 26

The knock on the door to Lew's office startled Osborne, who had just poured himself a cup of coffee and was in the midst of pouring one for Lew. He turned to Lew with a questioning look.

"Who is it?" she called from where she sat behind her desk, busy with reviewing emails that had come in overnight.

"Bruce," said a voice from behind the door. Osborne pulled open the door.

"Bruce!" Lew got to her feet. "It's seven o'clock in the morning. What are you doing here so early?"

"I couldn't sleep. Got incredible results in late last night. Chief, you won't believe the DNA matches. I was so excited that I finally got up at five, went by the office to be sure I hadn't imagined things and decided to drive up here with the results."

"I appreciate that," said Lew. "But you could have phoned and emailed—"

"But then I couldn't see your face."

Lew laughed as she beckoned Bruce over to the table near the windows where the morning sun was flooding in. Icicles dripped on the pavement outside. If you didn't count the frigid temperatures outdoors, the combination of sunlight and Bruce Peter's good cheer was making for a very pleasant start to the morning.

"Okay, okay," said Lew as if she was trying to calm a Labrador Retriever, "let's all sit down over here and see what you got. Doc, pour this man a cup of coffee, would you please?"

"Lots of cream and sugar, if you have it," said Bruce, slapping a folder on the table as he pulled out a chair.

Osborne found himself chuckling. Bruce Peters might be a skilled forensic technician in his mid-thirties, an expert on grim matters, but at the moment he was as hyper as a ten year old who has just landed his first muskie.

Bruce leaned over the file he had laid on the table before him, eyes gleaming as they searched Lew's face. "Got a perfect DNA match with Charles Mason, okay?"

"Ouch," said Lew. "Guess I hate to hear that. So much for his wife's insistence he was out of town when the break-in occurred."

"Hold on. Got the same perfect DNA match from the national criminal database —a convicted felon in California who walked away from a minimum-security prison three months ago. *Richard* Mason is his name. Goes by 'Dick' and he's got a long rap sheet of white-collar crime. Forged checks, counterfeit checks, embezzlement, identity theft and ... tah dah! ... computer fraud."

"I'm confused," said Lew. "Just last night Beth Hellenbrand did a public records search, which turned up divorce records on Charles who appears to have been living in Minneapolis. But are you saying that Charles is really ... Dick?"

"Hold your horses, Chief, I'm not finished," said Bruce. "Next I compared the fingerprints on record for Dick Mason with the ones I took yesterday from Charles. *No match.* I also have a printout in my folder here of assorted mug shots of Dick Mason, which may be very helpful."

"The bottom line?" asked Lew. Osborne walked over to the conference table where Bruce was laying out the photos.

"The two are brothers," said Bruce, slipping photos from his file. "Identical twins." He turned one photo over.

"This fellow is at least fifty pounds heavier than Charles," said Osborne, "but I see definite similarities in the configuration of the skull." Years as a dentist had honed his ability to visualize the bone structure hidden beneath jowls and sagging skin.

"You have a better eye than I do, Doc," said Lew, poring over the photo. "This guy doesn't look at all like poor skinny, pale-faced Charles."

Bruce sat back quiet in his chair. "People change over time. I checked the records on Dick Mason and my guess is we'll find them to be the same height, blood type, everything except the fingerprints and the weight."

"So why," asked Lew, speaking slowly, "would Charles Mason's brother leave a DNA sample that would implicate his brother?"

"That is the question, isn't it," said Bruce. "I will tell you one thing, though—the average person is not aware that identical twins do not share the same fingerprints. Whoever said that criminals are brilliant?" Bruce grinned, "at least not as smart as me. Seriously, DNA is the gold standard today. Most lab techs in law enforcement would have stopped with the DNA match."

"Deliberate sabotage, you think?" asked Osborne.

"What time is it?" asked Lew.

"Time to call Charles Mason," said Bruce. "I will bet you a fly fishing trip to Jackson Hole that he and his brother are behind the computer fraud at the college."

Charles sounded mildly surprised when he got the call from Chief Ferris an hour later. "Certainly," he answered when she asked him to come in to the police station. "I'll drive right in if you wish."

"No, Charles, ten o'clock is just fine," said Lew. Beth had called to say that the divorce papers and legal files would be arriving by nine thirty and Lew decided it would be good to have those documents on hand during the meeting with Charles.

"Think he'll try to run?" asked Osborne when she was off the call.

"That wouldn't be smart," said Lew.

"Smart does not take money from a wife and disappear."

"Now wait, Doc. The divorce papers stated that he left those women—not that he disappeared. After all, he did get served with divorce papers. I don't think he'll run … yet.

"I would like you and Bruce to sit in on my questioning of Charles. The lawyer's documentation will be impeccable should he deny the marriages and the lawsuits. Bruce, do you have the time?" She glanced over at Bruce.

"Wouldn't miss it," he said.

With two and a half hours to go until ten o'clock, Osborne busied himself making phone calls in hopes of finding someone who knew Walter's niece while Lew called Ray and arranged for him to take Bruce along when he checked the area around Walter's shack for footprints.

"Bruce," she had said, "see if you can find fingerprints, bullet casings that may have been overlooked because of cracks in the floor—any evidence that might help us identify the party who killed the old man. Todd was working the crime scene when he got called away—one of his kids got injured playing hockey.

"Here," said Lew, handing him a file, "I have his notes on what he managed to cover. If you could make some headway that would be helpful. It's frustrating how shorthanded we are but that will change after the tournament, thank goodness. But tell Ray you need to be back before ten."

Bruce returned a good twenty minutes before the meeting. "Good news and bad news, Chief," he said. "That shack is a challenge. I've lifted a number of prints to sort through later though initially they look to be from the same individual. Oh, and I did find one bullet casing that had rolled through a crack in the floor. That's worthless unless we find the actual murder weapon.

"I'll doublecheck the prints to see if I can find any that differ from the victim's but right now it looks to me like whoever it was who shot the old man just walked in and walked out."

"Todd missed the casing? That doesn't make me happy."

"A lot of debris between those floor boards, Chief Ferris. *Years* of debris, plus it was under some bloody matter—tissue." On that grim note, he paused.

"And the good news?" asked Lew.

"Oh that," said Bruce with a wide grin. "While we were out there your friend, Ray, got a call on his cell that his ice shanty is one of four finalists in that contest they got going. A crew from the TODAY SHOW is flying in later today to cover the final judging for both the international ice fishing tournament and the shanty contest. He's pretty excited."

"I'll bet he is," said Osborne.

"That's terrific news," said Lew. "But did Ray say if he found any tracks in the area?"

"Not yet, but he's planning to go back this afternoon. They asked him to stop by the officials' tent before lunchtime to fill out some paperwork for the final judging."

A gentle knock at the office door changed the expressions on everyone's face.

Charles entered. "Good morning, Charles," said Lew in a brisk tone. "Please, take a seat here at the conference table."

Charles walked over to sit down across from Osborne. Bruce took a chair next to Osborne at the round table. Lew sat in the center facing all four and with Charles to her immediate left. She pushed her chair back and turned so she could speak to him directly.

"Charles," said Lew, setting a hand on the manila envelope that had been delivered, "we know about Linda, Wendy and Kathleen."

"Oh." With a heavy sigh, Charles slumped back in his chair. He looked grayer than ever and his ponytail hung limp over his left shoulder. "I guess it was just a matter of time."

"As of late yesterday, we were convinced you were a bigamist," said Lew. "But just this morning we got records from your most recent wife's lawyer that indicate your divorce was final last August. Would that have been *before* you married Patience?"

"Two days before," said Charles, shifting in his chair and clearing his throat.

"You know you have the right to a lawyer if you wish," said Lew. "You don't have to answer my questions ... Would you like me to read you your rights?"

"That's fine. They've been read to me before. I know them by heart," said Charles. "Not necessary."

"All right, then," said Lew, reaching for one of the documents from the law firm. "We know that Kathleen would not agree to the divorce until you repaid one hundred thousand dollars that you took from a joint savings account two years ago. How did you manage to repay that amount? That's a lot of money. Did you take the money from Patience? Did she give you that money?"

"I had help from my family."

"Dick?"

Charles went from gray to white. Osborne thought he might pass out.

Lew gazed at Charles for a moment before saying, "Charles, we know all about Richard. We know he is an escaped felon with warrants out for his arrest. Tell us where he is."

The man leaned forward to put his elbows on the table and

cover his face with his hands. After a long moment, he raised his head and said, "If I turn my brother in—he'll kill me. He will kill Patience and, if you get in his way, he may hurt one of you sitting at this table.

"My brother has no conscience. He has infected my life since we were kids." He spoke clearly, simply and Osborne believed him.

CHAPTER 27

"**O**ur parents were killed in a car accident when we were four years old," said Charles. "Christmas Eve some woman driving drunk after an office party swerved and hit their car head on. My dad had just got his paycheck that day and my folks had been out Chrismas shopping or we would have been in the car, too.

"There were four of us kids. Dick and I are the youngest. At first one of my mother's sisters tried to take care of us but she couldn't afford it so my two older sisters stayed with her and we were put in foster homes. Dick and I grew up with different families. I was in two different homes over the years but Dick must have been in a dozen. He was always getting kicked out."

"Why was that do you think?" asked Lew.

Charles shrugged. "He's a mean sonofabitch. I suppose sometimes he was put with the kind of people who take kids in for the money so they deserved what they got. Most times he was mean to the other kids, to the foster parents, to family pets. But to hear Dick tell—it was never his fault."

"Growing up, did you two go to the same schools?" Lew asked.

"Sometimes. Grade school, yes. Different high schools because they kept moving Dick around. We were always in touch, though, through our sisters." Charles sighed, "Even though he got kicked out a couple times for fighting, Dick pretty much breezed through high school taking shop classes and stuff. He's good with his hands—can build anything.

"I managed to finish." Charles gave a sheepish look. "The only class I ever got a decent grade in was art—so these past few months have been really nice for me." He spoke with regret as if knowing that his days as an artist were over.

"Yeah, my brother is a lot smarter than me. A real whiz when it comes to numbers and computers." Lew made a note on the pad in front of her. Osborne glanced over at Bruce who gave a slight nod though he didn't take his eyes off Charles.

Charles' voice was subdued as he spoke, so much so that Osborne had to strain to hear him. It was as if he was confessing rather than describing his brother.

"In our late teens, after high school— neither of us went to college—and when we were out on our own, I didn't see Dick for quite a few years. I've always stayed in touch with my sisters, who told me he'd gone west where he got arrested for forging checks and hoodwinking whoever hired him—mainly hardware stores, I think. He's been in jail or prison off and on for years. During one of his stints in prison, he studied accounting, which he's good at. But," Charles shifted in his chair, "his real talent is conning people ... women especially."

Lew resisted the urge to comment: "Like you, bud."

"You can see from the divorce records you got there," Charles waved a hand toward the documents on Lew's desk, "that I've always stayed with low-paying jobs like being a sales clerk or stockperson in a warehouse. Construction, I'm good doing interior detail stuff, which is how I met Patience."

"Let's go back to your remark that your brother is good at conning people," said Lew. "Wouldn't you say that you're pretty good at that, too?"

Charles' face reddened. "See, I'm not proud of it, but ever since

I was a kid, women have liked me." He gave an apologetic look around the table. "Not sure why but something seems to work."

"Oh, I think you know why," said Lew in a dry tone. "Let's not kid anyone around here." Osborne hadn't heard her speak with such an edge before. He was impressed.

Charles looked uncomfortable. "Well, three wives later, I'm ashamed to admit that I have behaved miserably with women who deserved better." He shook his head.

As if he had made up his mind about something, Charles straightened up in his chair. He looked at Lew and said, "I'm not a very nice guy, I will give you that. But Patience is my first real chance to change things. She loves me. And she is kind. I've never known a human being so ... kind."

"Then why on earth would you steal from her?" asked Lew. "I admit I'm guessing here but from what we've learned about you and your own statement that she thought you had—makes me wonder if she was right."

"She was right. She was very, very right." Charles sat silent and the people in the room waited. Finally he gave a weak chuckle, "I've been stealing from women all my life. I stole from my sisters before my parents died. I stole from my foster mothers, I stole from teachers.

"Dick, too. We worked together. I would find some woman who had money, charm her, marry her—and get in touch with my brother. Dick would show up and together we would run a scam. He's the one who knows how to get into bank accounts or fool around with checks. He would take the money, give me some and leave. It was a bad act but divorce isn't jail time. I was able to persuade my ex's that Dick forced me into taking the money so they never accused me of stealing—we'd divorce and I'd promise to pay it back. And, sometimes, I did pay some."

"You did this three times, you and Dick?" Lew tapped a pen

on her desk as she spoke.

"Well, there were a few girlfriends in there, too."

"And your brother had no problem taking advantage of the women? Obviously you didn't, either," said Lew.

"I didn't really love those women and he knew that. They were a convenient way to be safe, to have a decent life. After a while, I'd get bored or, you know, start up with someone else. Time to take the money and move on. Again, I'm ashamed to tell you these things but—"

"Why would you let him do that? Why would you let him just come in and ruin your 'decent' life?" asked Lew.

"He's in charge. Always has been. He knows how to hurt me—I learned a long time ago not to let that happen." Charles was silent. He cleared his throat. "When people tell you who they are, believe them. Dick told me once that he would kill me if I didn't do what he said. He is always armed and, like I said, good with his hands." Charles looked around the table: "If you don't know people who can hurt you, count yourself lucky. Very lucky."

"So he showed up here in Loon Lake? To run the same scam?"

"Worse than that. When he tracked me down here, which was a couple months ago, he needed a place to hide out for a while. Put together a new identity. Patience was out of town at a conference so I let him stay over at the house. That night we had a few drinks and I passed out. When I woke up the next morning, he was on her laptop in the den.

"Right away he could see that I had accessed one of Patience's accounts and moved some money."

"Ah-h-h," said Lew, "so you did that on your own?"

"I used it to buy the gold to make our wedding rings. I was going to pay it back."

"How much are we talking about?" asked Lew.

"Ten thousand."

"And she didn't know you took it?" Lew asked.

"Not at first. Then her accountant called to ask what she spent the money on. I tried to convince her that the bank made an error. That was right when Dick got here."

"So he demanded some of the money?" asked Lew.

"No, he didn't want the money. Actually, he had plenty of cash on him. I have no idea from where but he said he was willing to replace the ten thousand before she could accuse me of taking it—in exchange for ..." Charles voice trailed off. Then he lifted his head resolutely.

"So he gave me the money, which I deposited right away. I was able to convince Patience that the fluctuation in the account balance was a computer glitch and when she saw that the money was in there, she believed me."

"I think she *chose* to believe you," said Lew.

"Yes. She gave me a break," Charles voice was meek. "I don't deserve Patience. I know that. Better to have this all over than have the one genuinely good person in my life get hurt. Dick's spamming operation has already damaged the reputation of the college not to mention my wife. I'm willing to help put an end to this—but," Charles leaned forward, voice hardening as he said, "*you have to help me keep Patience safe.*"

"What exactly was the trade between you and your brother?" asked Lew. "Obviously you made it possible for him to hack in to the college system but how?"

"I gave him access to her laptop. He figured out Patience's password and got into the college network. All that spam that was sent from her email address—that was Dick. All the spam that's being sent today? The identity theft? The stolen credit card numbers? He has pros helping him. He told me it's an international operation and all he has to do is 'keep the door open.' The key to his whole operation is that the spam must come from a computer within the college system—that validates the offers, that's why the spammers pay him. The fact that some of the offers came from the office of the college president—"

"Like the discounts on textbooks?" asked Lew.

"Right. For Dick—that was stealing candy from kids."

"So he uses the laptop in your home first, then various computers at the college," said Lew, taking notes. "How often was he in your house?"

"Patience's schedule is very predictable. On the days that Dick wanted access because he couldn't get into the college for some reason, I would be sure to leave the doors unlocked. He would come by snowmobile, park back behind the garage —a trail runs back there—and let himself in. He never needed more than half an hour. But last week everything changed. May I have a glass of water, please?" Charles' hands were shaking.

"You know, don't you, that everything I'm telling you now will very likely get me killed."

"Maybe not," said Lew. "You give me enough information, I can lock your brother up before he hurts anyone."

"Yeah," said Charles, "but he always gets out, doesn't he." He sipped from the glass of water that Osborne handed him then set it back on the desk, though his right hand shook so hard he almost knocked it over.

"I know my faults but I also know that I have ... great affection for this woman I'm married to. Not sure I know what love is—but I care so much for Patience. Once Dick started the spam operation and I saw the damage it was doing to the college and to Patience, especially to Patience ... She has worked so hard to build that college into something that her father would have been proud of ...

Rocking back and forth, he spoke, looking as the memory alone might cause him to vomit any moment. Charles managed to get out the words, "I kicked him out last week."

"Dick," said Lew.

"Yeah, I told him enough was enough and he had to stop—he

had to leave town. No more using my wife to run this horrible fraud. I expected a repercussion of some kind but for God's sake, the man made over half a million!"

Charles paused, head down, then said raised his eyes to Lew and said, "I thought I had talked him into taking it all the money and leaving. 'Take it all, every penny,' I said. 'Just get the hell out of here—now, today. Please.' I made it clear the money was all his. He seemed to agree.

"Then the break-in while I was gone. He knew I was going to be away that weekend and he must have figured he had one more opportunity to make money. But when he got here and found that someone had substituted a different laptop and changed the password and email addresses ... I'm sure he assumed it was me."

"I don't understand why he would leave the obvious—that semen on the bedclothes?" asked Bruce. "He knows that's easy to trace through DNA. And it is your house, after all. Your marital bed."

"I said my brother is smart, I didn't say he's brilliant. He was angry that I tried to stop him His revenge? Make me take the rap for his spamming fraud. That mess on our bed was disgusting but it would make it look like I never went to the conference in Milwaukee. Maybe leave Patience thinking I had had another woman in the house. Who knows—but he did it to make it look like I had been there.

"With my record," Charles pointed at the divorce documents, "who would believe me? Even if Patience did—no one else would. Why would they? I come across as a liar and a weirdo. One hell of an easy target and brother Dick knows it."

"Where is he right now? That's the question," said Lew.

Charles stared at her. "I haven't heard from him since the break-in but that doesn't mean anything. I'll do my best to help. I have to—for Patience." He glanced over at Lew, "Am I under arrest this morning?"

"You're an accomplice to computer fraud," said Lew. "I have to. Sorry."

"Would you let me tell Patience—in private?"

"Of course," Lew said. "But first, since we know your brother is entering the college at random times to work on various computers, we must stop him. Where can we find the man?"

"I don't know where he is living. In all these years, whenever he's been around, he has never told me where he sleeps. Dick is always on the run from somebody. Half the time it's the Feds, so he says it's best if I don't know. Hell, I don't argue with the man—I don't want to know."

"How does he get in touch with you then?" asked Lew.

"Prepaid cell phones. Can't be traced."

"We know all about that," said Bruce in a frustrated tone. "At least around here that's the case."

"Charles," said Lew, "that art seminar you attended. Did you happen to buy any art supplies while you were there?"

"I got some new oil paints. Why?"

"Do you have the receipts?"

"I do. Patience's accountant insists I keep all those. For when my art sells," he snorted. "Fat chance for that happening."

"Good, that's all I need to know." Charles gave her a curious look but Lew volunteered nothing more.

Bruce slid a photo across the table. "Mr. Mason, is this your brother?"

Charles looked down. "Yes, that's Dick. Bigger than me, isn't he? Always has been. Bigger, stronger. I'm the runt. But I am better looking, aren't I?" He gave a sad smile.

CHAPTER 28

A short time later, after arranging for Patience and Charles to meet in private in the large conference room down the hall, Lew locked the door and returned to her own office.

"Time to set a trap?" asked Osborne as she walked into the room where he and Bruce were waiting. A nervous worry gripped him as it always did when he knew Lew was about to put herself in danger.

"Maybe," said Lew. "Thanks to Beth and Dani, we know the pattern: even though he has never been seen, the network activity indicates that Dick Mason has been somewhere on the college grounds every other night. Assuming he keeps to that schedule, if I can have surveillance in place tomorrow night between nine and midnight—"

"But you are so shorthanded," said Bruce. "Why don't I check with my boss and see if we can provide back-up from Lincoln County?"

"No, but thank you for the offer, Bruce," said Lew. "I want the FBI to take over ASAP. Now that we know who is behind the computer fraud—which really should have been their job—the least they can do is provide the manpower to nab the guy.

"Given that he is a fugitive from a federal prison in California and likely other warrants have been issued for his arrest—dammit, this case belongs to them.

"I've had it," said Lew, slamming the file she was carrying down on her desk. "I'm tired of going with five hours of sleep every day and I'm tired of our department doing a half-assed job for the people we're supposed to be working for. You know?"

It wasn't a question but a rhetorical demand and Osborne had a flash of sympathy for the FBI bureau chief who would be on the receiving end of her phone call.

"As far as I'm concerned, screw their case in Ironwood, Michigan. It can't possibly be as serious. This is a multi-million dollar scam happening under our noses. If the regional bureau won't come through, I am prepared to go higher."

"You know, Chief Ferris, you are absolutely right," said Bruce, looking up from where he was sifting through the legal documents sent over from Minneapolis. "Not only is this a federal case but I know several FBI officials to call if the regional guy blows you off."

"Good, but that doesn't solve another problem I have with this case," said Lew, striding back and forth with a grim look in her eye. "What if they agree to take over and take so goddamn long getting up here that Mason gets away? He has to know we're closing in on him."

"Right again," said Bruce.

"That does it. I'm calling the regional bureau chief as soon as we're finished here," said Lew. "If he doesn't have agents heading this way by morning—I'll have his career."

"In the meantime, Dani and I are planning to monitor the network tonight. I don't want to take the chance that Mason might change his routine and try to access one of the computers tonight."

"Is Todd available to help you out?" asked Osborne. "Because you need back-up if Mason shows. Let me stay with you."

"I'd offer, too" said Bruce, "but I don't have the credentials unless you want to deputize me."

"Doc and I will be fine," said Lew. "But thank you for offering. I'll check with the sheriff's department but with the tournament main events scheduled for tonight, he may not be able to spare anyone. I know Todd isn't available. I've got both Todd and Roger working twelve-hour shifts ending late tonight."

Lew checked her watch, "I hope Patience and Charles finish up soon. I want to call the FBI but not if I'm going to be interrupted—" At a knock on the door, she put a finger to her lips, then said, "Come in, please."

"Chief Ferris?" asked Patience, poking her head through the doorway, "do you have a minute?"

"Certainly, come right in," said Lew. "Would you prefer to meet in private?"

"No," said Patience, glancing over at Bruce and Osborne, "everyone here knows the situation. May I sit down?"

Before Lew could answer, she took the chair in front of Lew's desk. She seemed oddly composed: her features were relaxed and she walked with a new air of confidence.

"First, I'd like to say that Charles has told me everything and— you may find this strange—but I'm relieved. I've known in my gut that something was really, really wrong but now that the worst is out in the open ... Well, it helps to know the enemy, doesn't it?"

Patience offered a soft smile as she spoke. Her voice was calm, almost musical and she held herself with a grace that Osborne had not seen before.

"I'm very sorry things are turning out this way," said Lew.

Patience raised a dismissive hand. "You know, I am convinced we can work this out. I'm willing to post whatever bail the judge feels appropriate so Charles can be released in my custody. He promises to stay with me—at least until we know what we both want."

"And he is cooperating fully with our investigation," said Lew.

"Charles may have made some foolish mistakes but he isn't an out and out crook. After all, the money he took from me he was planning to spend on us. And he is a sweetheart. He isn't domineering and cold like some men I've known."

As she spoke, Osborne thought of her father: big, bombastic, bullying.

"Here is what I've decided," Patience was saying. "Since I'm willing to spend hundreds of thousands from our family trust on Wheedon Technical College, why not spend some of that money on ... on me and Charles? Maybe I can afford to be selfish for a change. So we're going to go into couples' therapy and see if we can work things out—even if Charles has to spend some time in prison. You know, I've never seen a therapist. Kind of looking forward to it."

She paused and looked around at each of them, "You people must think I'm absurd."

"I think you'll feel better knowing all the facts and giving your marriage a try," said Osborne. "I went through therapy during rehab at Hazelden and it changed my life. None of us are perfect."

"Speak for yourself," said Lew with a grin. Her face turned sober as she tipped a pen back and forth in her fingers. Osborne could see her deciding whether or not to speak. "Patience," she said finally, "at the risk of making things even worse than they are at this moment, I feel like I must warn you. Very likely Charles is a compulsive womanizer. I don't know that you—or therapy—can change that."

"I am very aware of Charles' emotional weaknesses," said Patience. "When a person grows up without a strong mother—or a warm mother figure—that can happen. I know how that works. Still, worth trying. Don't you think?"

"As long as you know what you're getting into," said Lew.

"Thank you, everyone. I appreciate the support."

"Patience," said Lew, "I am asking the FBI to take over the case. You have inherited a brother-in-law who, as you know now, is a wanted felon. Dani and I will monitor the computer network one last time tonight but the federal agents will need to meet with you when they arrive. Just a heads up."

"Chief Ferris, have Beth or Dani ever seen Charles' brother on the campus? Do we know what he looks like? Is he really identical to Charles?" asked Patience.

"If you are worried that you may have mistaken him for your husband, I doubt it," said Bruce, walking over to hand her a photo of Dick Mason.

"To answer your question," said Lew, "No. So far the only men that have been seen on campus during the time Dani has been monitoring the system have been the maintenance crew. I was with her last evening and—"

"What time was this?" asked Patience.

"Just after ten last night, why?"

"The college janitors leave by six," said Patience. "It's in their union contract. I wonder who she saw?"

"Whoa," said Lew. "That's good to know. I'll get on that right away. Bruce, may I have one of Dick Mason's mug shots? I'm meeting Dani at the college at seven tonight and I'll run a photo by her.

"Will everyone excuse me now? It's imperative I get hold of the FBI. I'll need to brief them and that may take some time. Everyone except you, Dr. Osborne. I have one more question for you."

"Well, Doc," said Lew after Bruce and Patience had left, "right after I talk to the FBI, if there's still time, I'd like to sneak in a run by the tournament. I can only take an hour but I haven't seen it yet and I refuse to have done all this work around the tournament and not get at least a glimpse. Want to grab a snowmobile helmet and join me?"

"Sure, but why the helmet, Lew?"

"The front desk sent an email that Polaris just dropped off two new snowmobiles for the department. Every year they give us new ones to replace the ones they contributed last year.

"I need a trial run on one of the new sleds in case we have an emergency. So I thought we could ride over to the tournament and watch a little of the happenings. Maybe get a brat and a soda while we're there? Then we'll bring the sleds back and drive on out to the college for a few hours. And, if all goes according to plan, end the evening at your place?"

"Lewellyn, you deserve a break *and* a brat. Meet you back here at five o'clock."

If there hadn't been so much ice on the sidewalk, Osborne would have skipped to his car.

CHAPTER 29

The snowmobile trail snaked along the east side of Loon Lake, along wetlands of tag alder, tamarack and black spruce where homes had never been built. The brand-new Polaris sled that Osborne was on surprised him. It hugged the trail on curves and gave a low hum rather than the traditional roar.

Never having been a big fan of the "motorhead" sport, he hadn't expected to find the ride so enjoyable. But tonight the air was a delicious crisp-cold and his helmet, issued by the Loon Lake Police Department, fit comfortably, was designed for good peripheral visibility and, best of all, it was not fogging up. He had no trouble keeping Lew, who was outfitted in a black snowmobile suit with the bright red Loon Lake Police insignia on the back of her helmet, in plain sight.

Ten minutes from the station, they crossed Highway 17, forked left at the trail crossing and were climbing the hill that overlooked the ice fishing tournament. At the top, Lew pulled to one side of the trail and braked to a stop. Getting off her sled, she walked back to Osborne, lifting the plexiglass face plate of her helmet as she joined him.

"Oh my gosh, Doc, look at that. Have to be eight, maybe ten thousand people down there." Together they stood in silence gazing at the pageant below.

Two huge tents were brightly lit and teeming with people in boots, fur hats, snow pants and puffy winter jackets. Across the top of the tents, waving in the stiff wind, were the colorful national flags of participating teams. The RVs of food vendors were parked outside the entrances to the tents and the aroma of bratwurst simmering in beer and onions drifted all the way up the hill to where Lew and Osborne were standing. A Leininkugel Beer truck was positioned next to the food vendors, its speakers blasting a Willie Nelson tune. Pools of light out on the lake illuminated the fishing areas and a steady stream of people could be seen wandering between the tents and the action out on the ice.

The parking lot was packed with vehicles, including row upon row of snowmobiles. Off to the right a quarter mile from where they were standing, Osborne could see the lights from the ice shanties, which had been set up in alternate rows.

"Gee," said Osborne as he searched for the big bluegill, "I wonder how Ray did in the final competition this evening? That ice shanty is so different from the rest—the judges had to love him or hate him."

"Give him a call on your cell phone, Doc. See if it's okay for us to ride over there and check it out. I haven't seen Ray's work of art yet and Suzanne is anxious to hear —hold on, my cell just went off."

As Lew unzipped the pack she was wearing around her waist, she yanked off her helmet and handed it to Osborne. "Yes? What! Beth, we'll be right there. Where are you? Meet you in the lobby to the main building. Don't do anything until we get there."

"Switchboard," said Lew into her phone in the next instant. "Marlaine, this is Chief Ferris. Emergency. I need backup at Wheedon College in the lobby of the main building. Got that? Get Todd and Roger out there, I don't care what they're doing.

"If you can't reach them immediately, call the sheriff's office. Call the EMTs. We got a possible shooting victim and a suspect who may be armed—they should approach with care. Same for Roger and Todd: *approach with care.*"

"Lew?" asked Osborne, stunned.

"That was Beth. She just got a garbled call from Dani that was cut off. She heard shuffling noises and what sounded like a gunshot then the phone went dead. Beth was at home but she's in her car now on her way to the college."

"You want us to ride back to the station for your car? Call for a squad car?"

"No, Doc. This trail connects to one that leads right to the college. Be faster by sled—especially with the traffic in town. But we haven't installed lights and sirens on these sleds yet so be careful at the crossings."

"Got it." Osborne hit the throttle and hoped to hell he could keep up.

Through the darkness, they sped. Twice other riders approached from the opposite direction but the trail was wide and Lew did not slow. A final stretch through the forest surrounding the college flew by. Twice Osborne took corners a little too fast but the sled grabbed and he managed to avoid tackling a tree headfirst. Determined to stay close behind Lew, he refused to consider the consequences of losing control.

Beth beat them to the college by less than a minute and was just entering the main lobby after jumping from her car so fast she left the engine running.

"This way!" she shouted as she ran into the administrative office where Dani had been monitoring the network. A purse was on the floor next to the desk holding a wide-screened desktop computer.

"Where is she?" asked Lew.

"I'll know in a second," said Beth, bending over the desk, her fingers frantic on the keyboard. "There, I see it. A computer in the auditorium box office is in use. Has to be the one.

"I told her and told her not to try to see who was online," cried Beth as they ran down the hallway. Both Lew and Osborne's boots were wet with snow, which made it difficult to run too fast without slipping and falling on the tile floor.

The box office was located to the right of a long bank of windows in front of which sat the cafeteria tables where students ate their meals. Beth flipped light switches that illuminated the cafeteria and turned on the spotlights over the outdoor eating areas used in the summer. Closed off for the winter, the outdoor dining area was lined with snow banks. Just this side of the snow banks and immediately outside the windows was a snowmobile trail that circled the school.

Osborne looked through the windows at an Arctic Cat snowmobile parked near the double doors into the cafeteria and shining bright red under the spotlights. A tall figure in a black helmet and black snowmobile suit was just swinging a leg over the sled and the sudden roar of a full throttled engine could be heard.

"Ohmygod, she's been hurt!" Beth was on her knees beside Dani, who lay on the floor just inside the office. One quick look at the girl and Osborne had one thought: CPR.

"Dani? Dani? Can you hear me?" he said, gently pushing Beth aside and brushing the girl's mass of curls back from her face. A long silver clasp fell to the floor.

"Looks like a bullet may have grazed her skull," he said, pressing his fingers against her neck. "She's got a pulse. She's breathing. Do we have anything we can use to put pressure on this wound? A scarf? Anything?"

"Here," said Beth, handing over her woolen gloves. "Will these work?"

"Yes," said Osborne, preparing to hold them tight against the girl's head until the ambulance arrived.

Lew, hovering over the stricken girl, said, "Dani, do you hear me? We're here. You'll be okay."

A groan and one foot shifted.

"Beth, you take the gloves and stay with her—press tight on that wound," said Lew. "The EMTs will be here any second. Don't move her whatever you do."

Lew turned as Todd burst through the door. "Todd, help Beth. Doc and I are after the suspect who's on a sled."

"But, Chief, your squad car—" said Todd.

"I got those new sleds. They're good." Lew was already moving towards the cafeteria and Osborne followed, trying to buckle his helmet, which he had pulled halfway off thinking he would be doing CPR. "If we're lucky, we'll catch him.

"Doc, out this door and around to the front. We'll get to the sleds faster on the snow." Stepping outside, Lew paused for a second to check the direction of the fleeing snowmobile. A single bouncing light could be seen just entering the woods past the parking lot. "Would you believe he's on the same trail we took out here? Let's hope something slows him down ... Stay close behind me if you can—and, please, don't skid out."

As their sleds raced through the night, Osborne struggled to remember where he had seen an Arctic Cat like the one they were chasing. He knew it had to be in the last few days. Was it up at the fishing tournament? Or driving by Ralph's Sporting Goods where they always have new sleds on outdoor display?

Wait—it was in back of that pick-up truck at the old Russian camp near Walter's. Now he remembered: Ray had commented on how it was one of the new racing sleds.

Great, thought Osborne. These Polaris models are work-horses—not racing sleds. Fat chance we have to catch this guy.

CHAPTER 30

Struggling to stay close behind the beam from Lew's headlight, Osborne was pretty sure Lew was right—they were backtracking the trail they had taken to the college. When they crossed Highway 17, he was sure. Fortunately there were only two cars in sight and they were a distance down the road.

Lew never braked as the runners on her sled ground their way across the concrete roadway. Osborne was within twenty feet and dodged a snow bank left by the plows to land back on the trail.

Half a mile down the trail, Lew forked left to head up the steep hill they had come down on their way out to the college. In spite of holding his throttle wide open, Osborne's sled slowed going up hill. Lew was gaining on the other rider even as Osborne fell behind. Weight was making the difference.

When they crested the hill, there was no stopping to admire the throng below. Lew flew down towards the lakeside with the red Arctic Cat less than a hundred yards ahead. Osborne could see people standing next to the trail where it ended at the tournament parking lot. Snowmobiles were parked at the bottom and Osborne hoped that no one would step into the path of the speeding sleds.

But the rider on the Arctic Cat swerved off the trail onto the snowy slope behind the tents with Lew gaining on him. Beams from their headlights bounced as they landed on the snow-packed temporary road that led off to the right in the direction of the ice shanties, standing out in the glare of spotlights.

Just beyond the ice shanties he could see dozens of snowmobiles scooting along the trails that crisscrossed the lake. The Arctic Cat appeared headed for a cluster of snowmobilers gathered in front of a small stage that had been set up, but the rider made a sharp left before reaching the bystanders to disappear between two of the ice shanties. Lew did not follow.

Instead, she dropped off the road onto the lake to follow an outside path ringing the display of ice shanties. A good bet as Osborne saw the Arctic Cat zoom from the rear of one of the little huts out onto the lake. Both sleds were now off trail with Lew maybe fifty yards behind.

Osborne had not made up the distance he'd lost going uphill. He struggled to keep Lew's headlight in sight against the competing beams from the other sleds.

The lake surface was treacherous with mounds of ice rocks and shards pushed up by wind and weather and hidden by the snow. The pockets of ice were uncompromising when hit.

He knew of too many riders who had been killed or injured when their sleds collided with mounds like these, which were impossible to see in the darkness until you were right on them. The same was true for patches of open water over springs in the lakebed, places that never froze over. No wonder snowmobile clubs posted signs featuring the universal icon for danger and reading "STAY ON THE TRAIL."

Osborne's sled bounced hard but landed on both runners. Then a rough bump nearly knocked him off and he had to throttle down to stay upright. He made a mental note never to do this again. The dark was all encompassing now as they had left the popular trails behind and were across the lake near Hogan's Landing, which was a small island of pine trees and one bar.

Guarded by submerged boulders, it was a famed honey hole for fans of smallmouth bass.

The headlights from the Arctic Cat and Lew were pinpoints ahead of him and they disappeared as they rounded the island. Osborne gunned his sled to catch up, hoping he wouldn't lose them.

Already he was worrying over what might happen if Lew caught up with the rider. Was she armed? Was she wearing her Sig Sauer nine millimeter even though she had considered their visit to the ice fishing tournament "a break?"

The figure he had seen mounting the Arctic Cat was tall, intimidating. Dick Mason's mug shots showed him to be a man of hefty, muscled build quite unlike his twin. And he was an escaped felon, armed. Osborne pushed on.

Lew saw something strange as she raced after the fleeing sled: he had been just ahead of her by less than a hundred yards—but he was gone. Vanished. She slowed and as she did so, her headlight caught the ripples in the black water ahead. Yanking hard to the right, she hit the throttle and felt her sled slide sideways before gaining traction.

The snow-covered stump never budged even though her sled hit it with enough force to send Lew flying from the driver's seat. Airborne, she thought, this is not good, and waited. She woke lying on one side, helmet still on. She tried each limb but nothing seemed broken. Sitting up, she pulled off her helmet to see where she was. In the distance, she saw nothing but darkness.

"Doc?" she called. She got to her knees, then her feet. As her eyes adjusted she saw that she was close to the shore of Hogan's Island, the Polaris sled crumpled nearby. She staggered out onto the lake, terrified that Doc had not seen the open water. After charging through twenty feet of deep snow, she hit a snowmobile trail and ran.

Rounding the island, Osborne's headlight shone on something that gleamed black: open water. Brakes screaming, he veered left. The sled stalled out and he jumped off, tearing at his helmet. He stared at the gaping hole of open water: eight feet wide and maybe twelve feet long. Large enough to swallow one, maybe two snowmobiles.

Without hesitating and refusing to think the worst, he pulled off his mitts and unzipped his suit, jamming his hand inside to grab his cell phone. His phone had a quirky way of going dark right after he opened it. He couldn't see the numbers to call 911. Trying, he mistakenly hit the button for Ray. In an instant he heard, "Yo, Doc, come on by—"

"Ray, call 911. Get the sheriff and dive rescue team. Lew's sled just went down in open water."

"Where?"

"Across the lake from you—just past the eastern end of Hogan's Landing."

Ray's phone clicked off.

Grasping the steering on his sled, Osborne moved the headlight beam back and forth across the water. Nothing moved except light ripples in the night breeze. The opening in the ice was long enough and wide enough that it had to be the result of a spring down below. He heard a slight burbling from underneath the ice. The sound of an engine dying?

No sign of Lew's sled. He looked towards the island shoreline. Darkness. He pulled off the snowmobile parka and holding it, he walked towards the hole in the ice. When he felt a quiver under his feet, he knelt and, holding one arm of the parka, he threw it ahead. Pushing it in front of him, he crawled closer and closer. When he felt the ice give ever so slightly, he stopped. Waited. If she surfaced, she could grab the sleeve, he could maybe pull her far enough up on the ice ...

A numbness took over as he refused to think that Lew's life could have come to this harsh end. Two minutes at most had passed since he'd stopped. From experience he knew people survive longer in icy cold water. Still, the window for life is a short twenty minutes and even then ... A shudder passed through his body.

Nothing to do but wait. He thought through all the scenarios that might make it possible for her to survive: she wasn't belted onto the machine, her helmet might hold some air but it would weigh her down and be difficult to remove if water got in. Worse, she was outfitted in heavy, padded snowmobile clothing ... the boots.

He pushed his face down into the snow. It isn't fair. He lost his mother when he was six. He lost Mary Lee. Now Lew. His tears made tiny pockets in the snow.

A tug on his right boot. Another tug and a familiar voice, "Doc, inch back slow. You are too close to that open water."

"My god, Lew, you're okay!" He pushed himself up on his elbows.

"Goddammit, Doc, I said 'move slow.' The ice is cracking in front of you."

"Okay, okay." Moments later he got to his feet, suddenly freezing in the night air.

"Oh, Doc, I've been so worried you wouldn't see the open water in time," said Lew as they embraced. "Here, put your parka back on before you freeze to death."

"I thought you went down," said Osborne, holding her tightly. "I couldn't see any sign—"

"Sheer luck. I swerved right just as the Cat went down and barely missed going in after him. But I hit something and got thrown from the sled. I think I blacked out for a few minutes. The sled is wrecked," she said, pointing towards the dark shadows

of pine trees. "I might have a concussion but otherwise I'm okay."
She tipped her head back to look up at him. "Are you, all right?"

"Just fine," said Osborne, his voice hoarse. He kept his arms
wrapped around her and held tight. "Just fine."

Within fifteen minutes, a large pontoon-like iceboat flew
towards them, traveling over the ice on a cushion of air.
Three divers, outfitted in black dry suits, hoods and masks leaned
over the sides as the boat hovered twenty feet from the hole then
dropped onto the ice. As they clamored off, strapping on scuba
tanks, Lew asked the driver, "How'd you guys get here so fast?"

"Chief Ferris, we have been on call all week. With all the
traffic on this lake and the vehicles, we've been waiting for
somebody to go through. You're our first call. We thought it was
you who'd gone through, Chief."

"I managed to avoid that little trick," said Lew. "But I was
after a suspect who did go down, I'm afraid. So you folks have
work to do here."

"Thank God, it's not you, Chief Ferris. That would be
a bummer."

To say the least, thought Osborne, still pinching himself
to be sure he wasn't dreaming.

Challenging though the conditions might be, there was
excitement in the dive captain's voice. Osborne couldn't believe it:
these people relish diving under the ice.

"The suspect—who was on a sled—went down about
twenty-five minutes ago. Think it's too late?"

"We'll do our best. This water is murky even in daylight.
My people have strong headlamps but it will be tough to see.
At least we know the site—that's usually half our problem."

"Excuse me," said Lew as the first diver disappeared into the
black water, "I have some people to check on." Sitting nearby,

Osborne listened as she reached Todd who, along with Beth, had followed the ambulance carrying Dani. "Oh, that's a relief," said Lew. "And Beth? Is she doing okay?" As Lew listened, her face relaxed. "Thank you, Todd."

Closing her phone, she turned to Osborne. "Dani has a nasty bump and a flesh wound but nothing more serious. The emergency room doc thinks the metal barette she was wearing deflected the bullet. She's been x-rayed and they are going to keep her overnight for observation.

"Beth has headed home but Todd is going back to the college to be sure the crime scene is well protected."

Osborne reached over to pat her hand. Good, Lew, that's one thing you don't have to worry about."

Forty minutes later and just as Osborne's feet were turning to ice in spite of snowmobile boots guaranteed to forty below, the divers pulled the body, still in its helmet, from the water. The rider had plunged into a tangle of sunken timbers where his sled had lodged between two logs, trapping one leg.

"Whew! I sure am glad I won't be on the salvage crew tomorrow," said one of the divers as he climbed back onto the iceboat. "It's a mess down there. Logs, debris. Guy never had a chance."

Back on shore, the tournament officials hurried to curtain off the First Aid area so the divers could deposit the body and make room for Osborne to officially establish time and place of death. No doubt the man had drowned but determining the cause of death would be left to the pathologist at St. Mary's Hospital where the body would be kept in their morgue.

As soon as the dive team had laid the body on a gurney and left the small room, Lew and Osborne approached to study the face. The rider was heavy-bearded but he had familiar cheekbones and flat grey hair the same shade as his brother's. The eyes that had charmed Dani were vacant.

"Lewellyn," said Osborne in a quiet voice, "I'm ninety-nine percent sure this is the fellow who tried to run me and Ray off the site of the old Russian camp down the road from Walter's place. Let's get Ray in here and see if he agrees. I *am* sure that's the same snowmobile we saw in the back of his truck unless everyone is driving red racing sleds."

But Ray was busy. "Chief, I'll be down as soon as I can. You know I checked with the switchboard and they said you were okay so—"

"So what's the hold up? I want to get the body moved and call Charles Mason in for an official ID. How soon can you get here?"

"Give me ten minutes. I won the contest—"

"Oh," said Lew, "you mean you got first place?"

"I did! I won First Place and I'm just finishing up with the photographers. Have to be here at the crack of dawn for an interview with THE TODAY SHOW. Oh, and Chief? If you reach Suzanne before I do, would you tell her she's got to get that grad school application in? Now. We have a deal."

Lew turned a happy face to Osborne. "Ray won the ice shanty contest. Looks like he'll be here when he gets here. That's okay," she said, giving a sigh of exhaustion as she sat down on a nearby chair, "I don't mind waiting."

CHAPTER 31

Morning came too soon but Osborne did not want to miss Ray's star turn with the television crew. Lew, too tired to even think of spending the night at his place, had headed home to her farm. Even though he hadn't gone to bed until after two that morning, when the alarm rang at six Osborne was up and pulling on layers of warm clothing: a perfect day for fleece, lots of fleece. Better to wear too much and peel down later.

He could hear the coffeemaker brewing in the kitchen and Mike was wheeling in circles, eager to go out—little did he know it was thirty below zero. Osborne had to chuckle as he watched the dog prance across the yard. Eager doesn't work when you have delicate paws no matter how much you need to pee. Osborne opened the back door to a dog very interested in lying by the fire.

Wolfing down cereal and a banana, he marveled at how good he felt in spite of four hours of sleep. He decided it had to be his profound relief that Lew was alive and well. Those moments of staring into the treacherous black water would stay with him for a long time.

The television crew had set up by the time Osborne arrived at Benny the Bluegill. The morning sky was just beginning to turn pale as a cameraman took B-roll of the exterior of the ice shanty, then crept inside to shoot Ray where he sat jigging over a hole in the ice.

Osborne noticed Ray was letting his beard grow back and he looked resplendent in a silver fox fur hat and black parka with a matching silver fox fur collar. Osborne suspected Ray had persuaded Ralph to open the sporting goods store early that morning in order to spend all his savings on the outfit—savings that were originally intended to get him through the winter. Yep, someone's neighbor better prepare to be hit up for a loan or two.

Hanging back by the crew's van to stay out of the way, Osborne watched the footage on a monitor along with a young woman who introduced herself as the producer's assistant. Alternately gazing into the camera and sounding quite relaxed, Ray demonstrated his depth finder with its shadow images of large black crappies circling his Swedish Pimple lure—sweetened, he pointed out "with the eye of a perch."

"Cool—the eye of a perch," said the producer's assistant. "Very cool. This will air in an hour," she said. "I'll make a copy for Mr. Pradt after we edit for time."

"I'm planning to patent Benny," said Ray with a satisfied air as he and Osborne drove out to the Russian camp right after THE TODAY SHOW had aired.

"Well, Bud," said Osborne, "you could not have looked more professional. Good show."

"Thanks, Doc."

When they arrived at the cabin that Dick Mason had renovated during his months of squatting on public land, Bruce Peters met them at the door. "Morning, fellas. Step inside—it's freezing out there. But do me a favor and stand right over here, will you?" Bruce pointed them to a small area that had been used as a kitchen.

"Bruce, are you moving to Loon Lake?" asked Osborne, surprised to see him.

"Nah, but I stayed over last night to watch the tournament judging, which turns out to be a good thing. Chief Ferris got me on my cell this morning—told me Dick Mason went through the ice and asked me to check this place out.

"I've only been here a couple hours but I've found plenty— got a twenty-two pistol that was lying on a table in here. Couple deer rifles, too. Chief Ferris says they found a .357 magnum on the guy's body. This pistol was recently fired and I'm going to bet ballistics can match the bullets to the ones that killed the old man. I found a bullet casing at the old man's shack that had rolled into a gap in the floor under the bed. So we got something to work with though I doubt there's any question Mason shot the guy."

"But what threat could that old man have possibly posed to him?" asked Ray.

"Remember your note from the old fella saying he found what you wanted in the garage?"

"Right," said Ray.

"Well, I checked that new shed out behind this building," said Bruce, "and found ..." He held up a red aluminum snowshoe. "You assumed he was referring to his own garage but he meant this one."

"Kathy Beltner's other snowshoe," said Osborne. "Walter knew we were searching for that."

"I'll betcha he must have been poking around over here and Mason saw him," said Bruce. "See the crow's nest on this place?" Bruce pointed overhead. "It's new and there's a ladder over there to access it. Mason may have used it to shoot a deer or two but he really used it to keep watch. His brother said that he never told him where he was staying because people were looking for him."

"Walter said he'd had an encounter with the guy. We suspected he was keeping an eye on him ..."

"No doubt Mason figured that out fast. Probably thought the old man would tell the Department of Natural Resources or the forest rangers that he was squatting out here."

"Too bad old Walter wasn't still playing hermit," said Ray. "Would've kept him out of trouble."

"But my best find," said Bruce, holding up two small metal devices, "are these jump drives. I just stuck one in my PC to check it out and there's a ton of personal data stolen from the college emails—the students responding to those fake offers. These, my friends, go straight to the FBI."

"Whoa, that will make Chief Ferris's day," said Ray. "Bruce, any reason Doc and I can't take a walk around the place? I'm thinking that since that snowshoe has shown up here maybe we can find some sign of where Kathy Beltner might have lost them or—"

"Go right ahead," said Bruce. "The outdoors is all yours."

Ray stepped outside and gazed in the direction of the swamp and the Merriman Trails. "Let's start on the edge of the swamp, Doc. For once, we haven't had any new snow these past few days. That might help."

The morning sun was high in the sky and as they neared the swamp, Osborne saw pink splashes sprayed out across the snow.

"Ray? Check this out but don't get too close. We need Bruce out here."

Standing a yard away, they could see where the rough trunk of an old aspen bore witness to Kathy Beltner's death. Only the impact of a .357 magnum can do that kind of damage.

Osborne had no doubt Bruce Peters would find blood samples and, if they were lucky, a few teeth, maybe even the slug that killed her. Ray studied the spot then backed away to the west. Nothing.

He walked up to the tree and backed away at different angle, each time going at least forty paces in each direction.

"Jeez, Doc," he said after the third try, "I still cannot figure out how Kathy got this far off the trail. Oh, wait, look here," he said suddenly, pointing down to a well-trod deer trail that ran along the edge of the swamp in the direction of the Merriman Trails. Thanks to the fact that deer are creatures of habit and multiple deer will follow the same trails over and over again—nosing out the original trails even when they have been buried under deep snow—this trail was wide enough for a human to traverse with ease.

After alerting Bruce to the evidence among the trees, Osborne and Ray set off along the deer trail. They trudged for over a mile to a point where the deer trail merged with the Merriman snowshoe trail for a quarter mile before turning further east.

"The heavy snow the night she was killed covered this deer trail or we would have found it sooner," said Ray as they explained their finding to Lew later that afternoon. "When Kathy set out, it was dark but not that much snow had fallen and the deer trail is so wide that it would have been easy to misread. We think she wasn't watching and made a wrong turn. Next thing you know she runs into Dick Mason, who was keeping an eye out for 'people looking for him.' With his brother turning against him and knowing old Walter might have put the word out—he was desperate. Poor Kathy."

Before he left to return to the Wausau Crime Lab, Bruce Peters was able to report what appeared to be a match between the blood samples on the aspen, two nearby trees and Kathy Beltner's blood type. Days later, a more accurate analysis would prove that the blood was indeed hers.

CHAPTER 32

"**B**ut I didn't!" exclaimed Dani, a hurt expression on her face—or at least as much of her face as showed under the bandage she was wearing. She was already in a bit of a pout since half her bountiful head of hair had been shaved, requiring the rest to be chopped back in order to give a little balance to her looks.

It was Saturday morning, the day after the funeral Mass for Kathy Beltner and Beth and Dani were meeting with Lew in her office. "I didn't go looking for who was online," said Beth, repeating the denial. "I'm not stupid, you know."

"Then what *were* you doing?" asked Lew.

"I was looking for Dickie to tell him I couldn't ride with him 'cause my boyfriend, Zach, would get mad—"

"Dickie being this man but with a beard, right?" asked Lew, holding up one of Dick Mason's mug shots.

"Yes, but I didn't know that's who he was. He told me he was one of the janitors. But when I went to find him in the cafeteria, there he was on one of the computers the college keeps in the box office, he turned around and had a gun in his hand. That's when I slammed the door behind me and to tried to run through the cafeteria but ... I don't remember the rest. Just waking up in the hospital."

Dani's shoulders shook and Beth, who was sitting beside her, reached over to pat her on the back. "It's okay, Dani," said Beth.

"Chief Ferris and I—we've needed to hear from you exactly what happened. This makes sense to me. Does it to you, Chief Ferris?" asked Beth, looking over at Lew.

"Yes," said Lew, "it makes a difference knowing you didn't deliberately do what we had specifically instructed you not to do. A big difference. Did Beth tell you that Dick Mason is the same man who shot her friend, Kathy Beltner? I can't tell you how lucky you are—we are—that you're alive."

Dani wiped a tear from one eye and sniffled. "I know. My mom is still so upset."

"Okay, then," said Lew, pushing her chair away from her desk and speaking in a lighter, brisker tone, "where do we go from here, ladies? Beth, why don't you share with Dani the plan you and I have been discussing."

"Sure. Dani, Chief Ferris and I have met with Dr. Schumacher and we got the go-ahead to start an internship program for selected computer science students to spend time at the police department assisting with public record searches and other database projects."

"Really?" said Dani. "What about that consultant, Julie Davis, who showed us how once someone gains access to a directory of user names and passwords, they can take over an entire network? It was so amazing to learn how to trace the hackers. I'm really into that stuff now. Professor Hellenbrand," Dani turned to Beth, "is there any chance the college might bring our consultant here? I would love to meet her."

"That's an excellent suggestion," said Beth. Her eyes met Lew's and held.

"Dani," said Lew, "we have an offer to make." Dani's eyes widened. "If you will switch your major from cosmetology to computer science, Professor Hellenbrand, Dr. Schumacher and myself will vote to award you the first internship, six months of paid time in addition to academic credits, here at the Loon Lake Police Department. What do you say?"

"Sure," said Dani with a huge grin. "Yes, yes and yes. I would love to do that. Anyway," she dropped her eyes coyly, "you can't win customers as a hair stylist when you have a cut as bad as mine."

"Awww," said Beth, "it'll grow out."

"Maybe, but I kinda like it short," said Beth, tipping her head sideways and giving a shrug. Her eyes turned solumn. "I am sorry that I got so involved with that man. I-I should have known better ... you know? I thought ... I was so stupid ... I thought he had a crush on me." Her eyes filled with tears again. "I have a lot to learn about guys, I guess."

"Oh, Dani," said Lew, "welcome to the club. We all do."

CHAPTER 33

"Do I *have* to sit next to a man wearing a sweatshirt that says "Addicted to Quack?" asked Suzanne with a laugh as she, Ray, Lew and Osborne sat down to fish fry that Saturday night. A phone call from her mother with the news of Ray's success had prompted Suzanne to take one more day off work, leave the kids with their dad and drive north for the weekend.

"If a photo of me sitting here next to this razzbonya shows up on Facebook, jeepers. I'll never get accepted at the Cranbrook Academy of Art."

"But I'm a world famous ice fisherman," said Ray, "after THE TODAY SHOW aired yesterday, I got two calls from guys in Chicago who want to hire me to take them ice fishing. This is just ... the beginning, folks. And ... and ... I am also a builder of unique ice shanties. Just think, Suzanne," he said, "if you do get into Cranbrook, you can be my ice shanty designer. How 'bout that!"

"Let me get into grad school first, than I'll consider the offer, Ray." Suzanne laughed. "I am not sure how 'Designer of Ice Shanties' will play on my application when they ask me how I plan to use the MFA degree. But I am pleased that you—we—won. That's the best news I've had all week."

"And I have more good news," said Ray.

"You told us already. You're building ice shanties," said Osborne.

"Yeah, well that's seasonal. I have a better idea."

"That's always dangerous," said Lew with friendly grin.

"You know old Walter," said Ray, glancing around the table with a smug look on his face.

"Y-e-e-s-s-s," said Osborne, worried about what they might hear next. The niece he had reached had been quite cursory in her attention to funeral preparations for the old guy, basically agreeing to pay for a cremation, period.

"We'll figure out what to do next," she had said. "Just mail the ashes to me."

"Well," said Ray, "I called his niece after Doc talked to her and she agreed to let me take care of Walter, which I will do ... for free."

"And?" asked Lew.

"It will be a wildcat scattering over the land where Walter lived as a hermit all those years."

"Does the niece know that's your plan?"

"Nope. But no one's living on that property so what does it matter?"

"Why call it a 'wildcat scattering?'" asked Suzanne. "I've never heard that term."

"That's the funeral industry term for scattering ashes without permission."

"Ray, this not a good idea," said Lew.

"Chief Ferris, with all due respect, it is not against the law and I am talking about land where no one is living. Think what it will mean to Walter."

Everyone stared at Ray. "Okay, but what does this have to do with your new business idea?" asked Osborne skeptically.

"It's a start to a special service I plan to offer the bereaved. I'm calling it *Love, Honor, Cherish and Scatter*—and I will charge five hundred dollars to scatter your loved ones' remains. With permission," he added at the expression on Lew's face. "Only in locations where I have permission. Scattering ashes is big in the cities these days but no one is doing it up here ... yet. I see a real future in it."

After leveling a baleful eye on Ray, Lew shrugged and said, "You try my soul, sir. You try my soul. Now let's order. I'm famished."

Later that evening as Osborne sat in his favorite chair near the fireplace, feet up and his copy of TROUT MADNESS on his lap, he watched Lew working at the kitchen table. She was determined to read through Bruce Peters' reports from the Wausau Crime Lab before going to bed.

"Leave no paperwork undone?" kidded Osborne.

"Almost finished," said Lew without raising her head.

Her dark curls shone under the warm kitchen lights and he could imagine the fragrance of her skin even as he watched from a distance. She had a gift for stillness and he reflected on how, whether studying in silence or casting in a moonlit trout stream, she filled his life with a quiet eloquence.

Soon they would fall asleep, her breath warm on his back. Thank goodness.